INNOCENT

HEARTS

What Reviewers Say About BOLD STROKES Authors

❧

KIM BALDWIN

"Her...crisply written action scenes, juxtaposition of plotlines, and smart dialogue make this a story the reader will absolutely enjoy and long remember."—**Arlene Germain**, book reviewer for the *Lambda Book Report* and the *Midwest Book Review*

Hunter's Pursuit is a "...fierce first novel, an action-packed thriller pitting deadly professional killers against each other. Baldwin's fast-paced plot comes...leavened, as every intelligent adventure novel's excesses ought to be, with some lovin'. Even as she fends off her killers,...the heroine...finds the woman she wants by her side—and in her bed."—**Richard Labonte**, Book Marks, *Q Syndicate*, May 2005

❧

ROSE BEECHAM

"...a mystery writer with a delightful sense of humor, as well as an eye for an interesting array of characters..."—*MegaScene*

"...her characters seem fully capable of walking away from the particulars of whodunit and engaging the reader in other aspects of their lives."—*Lambda Book Report*

❧

JANE FLETCHER

"...a natural gift for rich storytelling and world-building...one of the best fantasy writers at work today."—**Jean Stewart**, author of the Isis series

"In *The Walls of Westernfort*, Fletcher spins a captivating story about youthful idealism, honor, and courage. The action is fast paced and the characters are compelling in this gripping sci-fi adventure." —*Reader Raves*, BookWoman 2005

❧

RADCLY/FE

"Powerful characters, engrossing plot, and intelligent writing..." —**Cameron Abbott,** author of *To the Edge* and *An Inexpressible State of Grace*

"...well-honed storytelling skills...solid prose and sure-handedness of the narrative..."—**Elizabeth Flynn**, *Lambda Book Report*

"...well-plotted...lovely romance...I couldn't turn the pages fast enough!"—**Ann Bannon**, author of *The Beebo Brinker Chronicles*

INNOCENT HEARTS

by

RADCLY*f*FE

2005

CREDITS
EDITORS: JENNIFER KNIGHT AND STACIA SEAMAN
PRODUCTION DESIGN: STACIA SEAMAN
COVER PHOTO: LEE LIGON
COVER DESIGN BY SHERI (GRAPHICARTIST2020@HOTMAIL.COM)

By the Author

Romances

Safe Harbor

Beyond the Breakwater

Innocent Hearts

Love's Melody Lost

Love's Tender Warriors

Tomorrow's Promise

Passion's Bright Fury

Love's Masquerade

shadowland

Fated Love

Distant Shores, Silent Thunder

Honor Series

Above All, Honor

Honor Bound

Love & Honor

Honor Guards

Justice Series

A Matter of Trust (prequel)

Shield of Justice

In Pursuit of Justice

Justice in the Shadows

Justice Served

Change Of Pace: *Erotic Interludes*
(A Short Story Collection)
Stolen Moments: *Erotic Interludes 2*
Stacia Seaman and Radclyffe, eds.

Author's Comments

Innocent Hearts is the story of two women who did not know there was a reason they should not fall in love. It is the story of the dreams they dreamed when all that mattered to them was the miracle of the love they had discovered together.

When I first wrote this, it was my intention to stir the reader's memory of that first blush of wonder that accompanies new love and to celebrate the beauty of passion between women. The second edition of this work, while expanded in preparation for a sequel, remains true to that aim.

My thanks go to Jennifer Knight for her sensitive reading of the work and her sage advice as to where I could "say more," to Stacia Seaman for editorial expertise, and to my readers on the Radlist and elsewhere for making every word a pleasure for me to share.

I was pressed to make my deadline, and Lee said, "Stay in Provincetown until you finish the rewrites," as she left to return to Pennsylvania, her work, and the day-to-day care of our lives. For the understanding and the patience, *Amo te.*

Radclyffe 2005

Dedication

For Lee
Today and Tomorrow

PROLOGUE

Boston
January 1865

Martha Beecher looked up in surprise as her husband rushed into the drawing room waving a piece of paper in his hand and shouting her name.

"My goodness, Martin! What is it?" She put her needlepoint aside and stared at him in alarm.

"It's from Thaddeus," he exclaimed. "He's talked to the wagon master of the next group leaving for the Northern Territory. We can join them, he says. He'll arrange everything as soon as we send word!"

She smiled at his joyful expression. There had been far too much sadness in his brown eyes of late, and although he tried to hide it, she knew he was unhappy. His enthusiasm now transformed his craggy features, making him look much younger than his forty-odd years. She wanted to share his pleasure completely but was gripped by a quick surge of anxiety as she thought of leaving her home for an unknown destination, surrounded by strangers for months while traveling over hundreds of miles of wild, unpopulated land. How impossible it had all seemed less than a year ago, when a letter had arrived from Martin's boyhood friend Thaddeus Schroeder, extolling the virtues of the unsettled West and the Montana Territory in particular.

Pure air, clear skies, and no crowds or stench of factories. Such a prospect was marvelous enough, but Thaddeus had also written:

The war that has divided the nation is a distant thunder here in the northern territories. Out here, any man can claim land just for the tending of it and make his fortune with the sweat of his brow. The newspaper is growing every day, Martin, just like our fine town, and I need a partner to help me run it. I want you to be that man.

At first, the idea of moving west had seemed nothing more than a wild dream. True, she had known for some time that Martin was discontented with his teaching position and equally dissatisfied with the changes in their life that the war and industrialization had brought. More and more people had flooded the northern cities from the impoverished countryside and the decimated South. They were looking for work in the factories that had sprung up everywhere, crowding the landscape and fouling the air. Crime and disease grew with the swelling population, making even her much-anticipated outings for shopping or socializing a cause for worry. Now, it seemed not a day passed without some new horror scandalizing the city and disturbing Martha's peace of mind.

Thaddeus's offer of a partnership on a newspaper and a chance at a new life had truly energized her husband. But what did they know of frontier living—they who had never been farther west than Albany? Soon after they'd received that initial letter, they visited the public library to study a map of the new territory.

Martha had to smother her horror at the sight of a few ink lines tracing a vast open area marked by very little evidence of civilization. "But, Martin, it doesn't even seem…settled."

"The towns are small and far apart, my dear," Martin had explained. "They started out as mining camps during the rush west to find gold. But they are growing larger every day."

"It's so far…"

"Only the last half of the trip would be difficult." He traced the route of the Oregon Trail with his finger as it passed through miles of territory marked only by one Army fort after another, oblivious to her reservations. "Thaddeus says about four months altogether, and the roads are good all the way into Nebraska. Of course, we would have to leave most of the furniture behind. But think of it! It's a brand-new country out there, just beginning to grow. With the Homestead Act promising land to any man who lives on it, a whole new world is going to spring up overnight. We could be a part of something grand, and the newspaper would be at the heart of it!"

As he spoke about their prospects, Martha realized he had already set his heart on leaving. She had tried then to share his enthusiasm and had gradually accepted that they would someday go. Now, looking at the flush of excitement on her husband's face, she knew the time was at hand.

"If we are to leave soon, we must settle on what to do about Kate," she said, struggling to hide her apprehension. "She is eighteen now and at the age when a girl should be marrying. How can we ask her to leave behind all that Boston has to offer for a life in a place we know nothing of?"

She knew how hard it would be for her husband to part with Kate, especially when it might be years before they saw their daughter again, and she saw his hesitation. "I'll go anywhere that makes you happy, Martin," she added, keeping her deepest fears to herself. "If you are happy, I will be, too."

But our Kate? Don't we owe her more? Who knows what type of men we might find in such an unsettled place. Kate is much too refined to become the wife of a shopkeeper, or worse, a...farmer!

Sitting beside her on the settee, Martin took her hand. "Martha, I don't know how I know, but I feel certain that this move will be right for us." His eyes clouded with concern. "But perhaps you are right about Kate. A young woman like her, giving up all of this—the dances, the parties, the finer things. Perhaps it would be too much of a hardship."

Doubt had crept into his voice, and Martha could not bear that. She took his large hand into her small one and said with determination, "Kate can stay here with my sister Ellen until she marries. She is almost of the age when she would be leaving us soon for a husband anyway. Perhaps it will be sooner, that's all."

He seemed comforted by her calm, strong words, and smiled again. "I suppose, after all, we should ask her."

Kate Beecher looked up from her book as her parents walked into the room. She was seated in front of the fire, the flickering glow illuminating her bold features and shimmering waves of shoulder-length hair. She smiled at them fondly, a question in her dark eyes. "You look like you have news," she said in her rich, full voice.

"Kate, darling," Martha began tentatively, "your father and I have talked at great length about this move west, and we feel that we should go." She glanced at Martin and took his hand. "We are not sure what lies ahead, but it will be very different from our life here. We are prepared to leave, but you're a young woman now, and this is the only life you have known. There are many opportunities here and comforts that you might never have in Montana. The theater, opera, your friends..." She trailed off and looked intently at her daughter, who seemed to be struggling not to interrupt.

"You two!" Kate exclaimed, her eyes alive with laughter. "Do you really think I would let you go without me and miss this great adventure? There is nothing I care for enough to keep me here, and no one I care for more than you. I want to come. I have always felt that this is *not* where I belong. Perhaps I shall find that I belong in Montana."

Martin was aware that his mouth was agape as he listened. *Not belong here? Preposterous.* Surely there was no young lady either more popular or more accomplished than his daughter. She had many friends and not a few would-be suitors. In addition to her dark-eyed, black-haired beauty, her wit and intelligence quickly won her acceptance in any circle.

Martha was dismayed by the excitement, so like Martin's, in her daughter's voice. Kate had altogether too much of her father's adventurous spirit. Martha blamed herself for allowing her to spend so much time with Martin as a child, accompanying him everywhere. Plainly she had not emphasized enough that Kate needed to prepare for a life as a wife and mother.

She had warned Martin that the college library was no place for a girl to be spending so much time. Although she accepted a young lady's need to read and write, she was concerned that Kate spent far too many hours alone with her books. When Martin had given in to their daughter's demands that he teach her about his photographic pastime, Martha finally had to put her foot down. A dark room filled with foul-smelling chemicals was no place for a girl, even if Kate was a "natural" at image making, as Martin so proudly proclaimed. If Kate needed something to occupy her time, she could learn needlepoint.

"There are not likely to be the prospects for your future on the uncivilized frontier that you would find here." Martha looked to her husband for support but found none. Bluntly, she continued, "There are so many promising young men here in Boston. You must think of that, Kate."

Kate spoke carefully, knowing her mother could insist that she remain behind. "Whether I am here or there, Mother, I will only make a match that feels right in my heart. I do not believe that love is dictated by geography. You know there is no one here for whom I have formed any attachment."

That was precisely what concerned Martha most. More than one suitable gentleman had accepted invitations to their home over the past year. Kate had received each one politely and had just as politely sent him on his way. But before she could protest further, her husband interceded.

In truth, Martin could not bear the thought of leaving for a new life without his daughter. "Are you sure, Kate?" he asked. "This journey will be long and difficult."

"Quite sure, Father," she answered, feeling the first thrill of adventure. "Make no mistake. I want to go!"

"Well then," Martin said with obvious relief. "It's settled."

Martha, her expression tinged with lingering uncertainty, said nothing as Martin took her hand and led her toward the door. Kate watched them go, struggling with the sudden urge to dance.

"The West," she whispered, hurrying to the window that looked out upon the cobblestone street that fronted the hedges enclosing their small, well-manicured yard. Just the word conjured a sense of freedom that she had despaired of ever finding in Boston, where it seemed that the shape of her life had been determined before she had even begun to imagine its possibilities. *She* had gone to the library too and, sitting alone at one of the long wooden tables, had pored over the very same maps her parents had likely studied. She'd repeated the names of faraway lands, imagining herself in the midst of wide-open spaces and wild countryside, so unlike the tight, narrow streets and crowded buildings that seemed to confine her every bit as much as her mother's plans for her future.

She traced a shape from memory on the window glass, an irregular outline of the Montana Territory, wondering who she might become on this journey. Whatever dangers or disappointments lay ahead, the future now held a promise that it never had before. She might have the opportunity to choose her own fate, and although she wasn't certain exactly what form she wished her life to take, she knew that it was something far different than what her friends hoped for. The staid and comfortable life that her mother envisioned for her and which her friends so readily embraced—married to a man who would provide for her and decide for her—filled her with a sense of unease whenever she contemplated it. Why that should be, she did not know either. But for the first time, she believed she would have the opportunity to find out.

"New Hope." She smiled, her heart light as she repeated the name of the town at their journey's end. "Oh yes. I want to go."

CHAPTER ONE

New Hope, Montana Territory
May 1865

M artin Beecher halted the wagon on the crest of one of the lower peaks of the eastern reaches of the Rockies and sat forward eagerly, anxious for his first glimpse of their new home. He looked down upon a sprawling town nestled in a valley carved out of rock, most surely by the hand of God. After weeks of traveling across seven hundred miles of plains and prairies, the majestic Continental Divide, consisting in some places of hundreds of miles of impassable peaks broken only by a solitary pass, appeared to Martin to be unassailable by anything other than a greater power. Yet far below, like a nugget of gold caught in a crevice of ancient stone, lay a tranquil sanctuary of scattered meadows still dotted with snow, a meandering river running high and fast with the melt from the towering ice-capped mountains, and copses of trees just beginning to green with the spring's warmth.

"There it is, Martha. We've finally arrived." He took his wife's hand. "And isn't it beautiful!"

Martha shifted on the rough wagon bench beside him, stiff from the lingering chill of the spring night barely past and bundled to the nose in a heavy wool blanket. She couldn't help but think that in Boston the tulips would be in bloom, whereas in the valley below, winter still lingered.

Kate pushed between them from the rear of the covered wagon, one gloved hand on each of their shoulders. Despite the cold, she was bareheaded and her glossy hair shone darkly in the bright sunlight. She shielded her eyes against the early morning sun and eagerly surveyed the scene before her. There were perhaps a dozen buildings, most constructed of milled lumber but a few of brick, on either side of a rutted dirt road that was clearly Main Street. Other clapboard structures centered on the main thoroughfare, and more than a few log cabins were scattered along the outskirts of town and farther into the foothills, where the early homesteaders had obviously settled. The rapid expansion that Thaddeus had spoken of was evident in the large numbers of structures under construction and the early morning bustle that was visible even from a distance. Wagons loaded with lumber and barrels of goods clogged the streets, and men on horseback churned up clouds of dust entering and leaving town.

"Is that New Hope?" Kate asked, her voice alight with an echo of her father's enthusiasm. "Are we here?"

She could hardly believe they had finally arrived. Once the decision had been made to leave Boston, everything had happened so quickly. Her father had resigned from the college and sold their house at a good profit. Her mother had donated most of their garments to several charities that provided for those who were displaced or left behind by the rapid pace of progress. Kate had helped Martha purchase simple, sensible traveling clothes for the entire family, although Martha insisted that they keep some of their "finer clothes" for social affairs or funerals, two events that well-bred ladies would be expected to attend even in a "frontier town." Taking Thaddeus's advice, however, they left almost all the furniture behind.

They set out from their home before the last graying snows of winter had melted from the streets with a plan to follow the warm winds west. Looking back, Kate wondered if they would have set off so readily had they any idea of the hardships that lay ahead.

The first segment of their journey had been relatively comfortable as they traveled by rail to Independence, Missouri. Since this was where the "regular" railroad service ended, it was the starting point for most expeditions heading to the western territories. In the previous year, 1864, a Congress still divided by the uneasy sentiments of war had passed the second Pacific Railroad Act, allocating funds for the construction of a transcontinental railroad. Shortly after the surrender of the Confederacy, the Union Pacific railroad began moving westward, rail by rail, but it hadn't yet been completed.

This meant that in Missouri, the Beechers had joined a wagon train, both for safety and to afford company for Martha and Kate. During the weeks that followed, they had many reasons to be grateful for Thaddeus's experience and the arrangements he had made in advance for them, especially since none of them, not even Martin, had ever been beyond the confines of civilized eastern society. Their trek across the midwest had been in a ten by five foot covered wagon that had barely accommodated the three of them, six stout trunks containing all their remaining worldly goods, several boxes of books, and a wardrobe of Martha's with which she refused to part.

As they slowly labored over narrow, rutted trails that often threatened to capsize their prairie schooner, spring had first overtaken, then threatened to pass them by, somewhere along the northern trail through the Great Plains. Even as they had traversed the flatlands and begun the climb toward the eastern slopes of the Rockies into the newly created Montana Territory, the last snows had not yet completely retreated. Overflowing riverbeds and streams made the last few weeks of their trek arduous for animals and humans alike.

The journey had been longer than expected, and they all agreed after a time that it was harsher than they had imagined. The Overland Trail was littered with the possessions of families that had not been as well prepared for the journey as they. Sadly, there were more than a few hastily erected markers remembering fellow travelers who, due to accident or disease, would never reach the land of promise they had so hopefully envisioned.

Even in the darkest moments, Kate had not succumbed to the sense of defeat she detected at times in her mother. She was aware more than once that her buoyant sense of anticipation combined with her father's unfailing optimism kept all their spirits from flagging. Now, with Boston receding into a distant memory, she looked down upon the tiny town and felt that her life was truly about to begin.

"Are we really here?" she asked again.

"Yes indeed, darling Kate," her father answered cheerfully. "At last—New Hope, Montana."

"I am so glad! I can't wait to meet the Schroeders. Do you know which is their house?"

He laughed, delighted by her eagerness. Perhaps he needn't have worried about her after all. He pointed toward the spire-peaked square clapboard building nearest them. "That's the church. Thaddeus said it was the first building they raised, and next to that the schoolhouse, I imagine. The Schroeders live somewhere near the center of town. I'm sure we will have no trouble finding them."

Kate did not see the stark simplicity of the town and the wild countryside as something to fear, as her mother did. Like her father, she saw a chance that her life might be more than she had been raised to believe it would be.

She thought about the last year of her life in Boston, the year that most girls her age remembered as the most exciting. It had not been for her. She had attended the required coming-out parties, the afternoon socials, and the debutante balls. She had been properly introduced and had made the proper connections. It had been pleasant, but somehow it struck her as frivolous, too. She found the conversations considered appropriate between young ladies and gentlemen dull and the attentions of would-be suitors tiresome. Perhaps here she would find that there was more substance and fulfillment to life than that.

She gripped her father's shoulder harder, saying, "And the newspaper office. Where is it?"

"I'm not sure, but it's the first place I want to see. Imagine it—one of the very few in the territory and soon to be the biggest," he pronounced proudly, throwing his arms around both Kate and her mother. "Just think of it!"

His excitement was so boundless, and so simple, that Martha's heart lifted at the sight of his pleasure. She returned his hug and said softly with more conviction than she felt, "It will be wonderful, darling. I'm sure of it."

"Yes," Kate whispered fervently. "It will be."

❖

Less than an hour later they located the Schroeders' house. Apparently, everyone in town knew them, and each other, because it had been simple to obtain directions from the first passerby. Martha was astounded at their reception. Thaddeus Schroeder's wife, Hannah, took them into their home as if they were long-awaited relatives.

"John! John Emory! You carry those bags upstairs while I get these folks something to eat!" Hannah bellowed merrily while herding the Beecher family into her living room.

She was a head shorter than Martha and almost twice her size, with a round face and twinkling dark eyes. She had none of the pampered look of the Boston matrons Martha had called friends, and her palpable energy was almost overwhelming.

Very much aware of being a sedate Easterner, Martha protested, "Oh no, really. We only stopped to let you know we had arrived." She looked to her husband and daughter for support. "I'm sure Martin can find us suitable lodging at the...uh...hotel."

"Don't see as how," Hannah responded earnestly, moving books and papers from the worn couch in the sitting area. "That hotel is sure to be full with cowboys in for the week's end or worse, and it's no place for you folks. You'll stay right here with us 'til you get settled. We've plenty of room, and a couple more mouths to feed is no hardship."

Kate recognized the look of consternation on her mother's face and took her arm, whispering softly, "Mother, I think we should accept Mrs. Schroeder's hospitality. It's been so long since we've slept anywhere but the wagon. Besides, it will give Father a chance to talk things over with Mr. Schroeder, too."

"That's right, my dear," Martin added. "I'm sure Thaddeus has suggestions for a place we might acquire."

Hannah nodded. "That he has. Now, I'll get busy heating water because I should think you'll be wanting proper baths along about now."

"Why don't you rest awhile, Mother, and I'll help Mrs. Schroeder in the kitchen," Kate urged.

The journey had taken its toll on all of them, but none so much as her mother. She had lost weight and seemed more fragile than Kate could ever recall. The hardships of the last few weeks on the trail, when there had been little to eat but salted meat and unleavened biscuits, seemed to have sapped the last reserves of Martha's strength. It did not occur to Kate when looking at her mother that *she* had been the one to change, growing stronger in body and spirit as the journey had progressed. She had been the one to handle the horses' reins while her father pushed the wagon from the deeply rutted, muddy trail and, sadly, she had witnessed death in all its cruelty without faltering. Sometimes she felt guilty for loving the challenges that were clearly so difficult for her mother. She patted Martha's arm. "Perhaps Mrs. Schroeder and I can make some of that tea we've been saving while we prepare the bath water."

"Yes, of course," her mother responded politely. She sank down onto the couch as if her legs could hold her no longer.

"Right you are. You come with me, child," Hannah said with authority and bustled out.

Kate followed, as eager for the chance to talk with Hannah Schroeder about the town as she was for the chance to soak in a tub for the first time in months.

Martha turned to her husband, uncomfortable in a home that was not her own and anxious that their presence would be an imposition. "Martin?"

He shrugged good-naturedly. "I guess it's decided."

CHAPTER TWO

A few days became more than a week before Kate's father, with Thaddeus's help, settled on a house on the southern edge of town. The dwelling was a modest but sound two-story wood structure with a wide front porch set a small distance back from the dirt street by a waist-high wooden fence with a swinging gate. There was also a large backyard with room for a small vegetable garden. Kate had never grown anything other than flowers in decorative pots on the windowsills in Boston, but she was certain she would be able to manage vegetables with a little instruction.

The inside was bright and spacious, with shiny wood floors, an open archway between the living room and dining room, and many windows. Kate was especially pleased to learn that there was a small room adjacent to hers on the second floor that she might use for her photography. Their new home was a brisk walk from the newspaper office and near enough to the other townspeople for Kate and her mother to socialize. Kate knew her father was worried that they would be lonely, but, as it turned out, his concerns were unfounded.

During their time at the Schroeders', she and her mother were besieged with visitors. Apparently newcomers, especially Easterners, were a rarity, and everyone wanted to meet them. Kate enjoyed herself thoroughly, taking advantage of the opportunity to learn all she could about her new home. She found the open, welcoming attitude of the townspeople appealing and their eagerness to answer her endless questions endearing, and she was soon accepting numerous invitations to tea and something on Saturday afternoons called a "quilting circle."

Martha, however, found the easy familiarity of the women a little unnerving. "My goodness, they're quite intense, aren't they?" she gasped after one particularly busy morning of entertaining in the Schroeder living room.

"Oh, I think they're wonderful!" Kate exclaimed. "I feel so welcome!"

"They *were* friendly," Martha admitted as she gathered up the remains of the tea biscuits they had served. "And so thankful for any bit of news. I can't imagine what it must be like waiting months to hear of events in the East." She sighed. "But I'll soon discover that, I'm sure."

"That's why what Father is doing is so important," Kate said enthusiastically. "It's the newspaper that will connect people, not just here, but in the entire territory, to the rest of the country."

Martha smiled. "I know you're right, and I *am* proud of him. It's just that this...place...will take some getting used to."

"It won't take long, you'll see," Kate said, kissing her mother's cheek. "And I'm proud of *you* for being brave enough to help him."

"Oh," Martha said with a small, deprecating laugh, "I don't know that I'll be much help, but I would never try to keep him from doing something that his heart called for him to do."

"And that's *just* why you're such a help." Kate reached for her shawl and bag, adding, "I asked John to show me more of the town this afternoon. We've been here for days, and I scarcely know what the place looks like. Would you like to come?"

"Not today, darling. I've had quite enough new experiences for one morning, thank you." Martha sank wearily to the sofa, sighing with relief.

Laughing, Kate leaned over to kiss her lightly on the cheek and said briskly, "All right. I'll be home soon. I promised I'd help Mrs. Schroeder with dinner."

John Emory Schroeder was seventeen years old—tall, strong, and sturdy. He was more than pleased to be strolling down Main Street with Miss Kate Beecher. He had never seen anyone quite as fetching as she, especially in that robin's egg blue dress that seemed to hint at her figure far more than anything he had seen the girls in town wearing. He didn't think for a minute that she might ever take notice of someone like him, but just accompanying her increased his stature in the eyes of all his friends.

"This here is the main street, Miss Kate. We've got a general store, right over there, next to the livery, and the bank across from that, of course. Down yonder is the schoolhouse, and—"

"Wait, John! Just show me as we go, please, or I'll never remember a thing," Kate pleaded with a laugh, pushing back her straw spoon bonnet to let the sun strike her face. Her mother would disapprove of the effects on her skin, but Kate didn't care. She couldn't stand to be hidden away. It was almost the first of June, and the air was still crisp and cool, so unlike the muggy early summer days she recalled in the city.

"Oh right, sure," he said, blushing to the roots of his sandy brown hair.

By the time they had walked the five blocks to the end of the central thoroughfare, Kate knew where women bought their dry goods and sewing materials, where the children went to school, and where the men from the surrounding ranches came to have a drink and spend their wages on a Friday night. Turning back, she was struck by the efficiency and order of the small town. Every need was met, simply and without embellishment. The street was clean and the board sidewalk sturdy, and all the faces she passed were kind and friendly.

"Let's rest awhile, shall we?" She brushed off a place to sit on the bench in front of the dry goods store. "It's so beautiful today, I don't want to go back inside just yet."

"Why, uh, okay," John said, at a loss for words.

He sat down beside her on the bench and stretched his long legs out in front of him. He swallowed self-consciously several times, but when it became apparent that Kate did not require him to converse, he relaxed. It seemed she hadn't noticed his discomfort, and he was thankful for that.

Kate was so engrossed with absorbing every detail of her new home, she paid little attention to her companion. Everything was so different, right down to the hard-packed earth of the street before her. Gone were the cobblestone roads and fine horse-drawn carriages that she was used to seeing. These common sights had been replaced by plain, board-sided wagons and heavy draft horses, accustomed to pulling loads of supplies or stubborn stumps, as their owners required. The timbered houses, though carefully tended and built to last, were a far cry from the stone townhouses where Kate and her friends had lived.

Despite the stark utility of the place, she sensed an air of vitality and vigor she had not noticed in the staid surroundings of her former home. A steady stream of ranchers and homesteaders poured through the town, loading wagons with supplies or off-loading their goods. Men called to one another as they led horses in and out of the livery, and women bustled in pairs along the board sidewalks, laden with parcels. She couldn't help but feel a thrill of excitement to find herself indeed a part of this strange new world.

She watched one of the young cowboys who had been passing by all morning cross the street to the blacksmith's opposite her. She was coming to recognize the purposeful gait and easy carriage that all the men seemed to have. Following the tall, lanky form clad in rough denim as he ambled toward the corral, she was struck by the unusual refinement of the deeply tanned features. As he swept off his hat to wipe a sleeve across his brow, she caught sight of thick, blond hair held back with a dark tie.

"Oh! My goodness," she cried in a startled voice. "That's a woman!"

"Huh?" John roused from his reverie. He had been nearly asleep in the warm sun. "Who?"

Kate pointed in astonishment, quite forgetting that it was rude. "Right over there."

"Oh, that's just Jessie," John said dismissively. "Her mare threw a shoe this morning, and she's coming to get her, I reckon."

Kate stared openly at the woman, who was deep in conversation with the blacksmith, one booted foot leaning on the lower board of the railing that fronted the corral. What startled Kate even more than her attire was the sidearm holstered neatly against her muscular thigh.

"She's wearing a gun!" Kate declared, amazed. She should have been scandalized, she supposed, but she was simply too surprised to be anything but curious.

"Why, I guess she'd better, riding into town alone, what with the way things are out on the range," John said matter-of-factly. "Settlers are fighting mad about expeditions crossing over their lands on the way to the Oregon gold fields, and my father says the miners are violating the treaties with the Indians, too. People are starting to get riled, and the marshal can't be expected to be everywhere, you know," he proclaimed with authority, echoing the words of his father.

"Yes, but—well, I mean—who *is* she?"

"I told you. Name's Jessie Forbes. She has a ranch a few miles out of town. Does right well, too, so everybody says. She doesn't seem to have any trouble selling her horses. I wish I could get one of hers," he said wistfully, "but I'll never have enough money."

"She has a ranch?" Kate said, eyes full of wonder. "You mean she *owns* it?"

"Well, I reckon so, since her father died a ways back, and she's the only one left."

Kate stared at the woman, whose features were shadowed at the moment by the wide-brimmed Stetson that she wore. Now that Kate looked carefully, she could see that the body was not that of a young man. Jessie Forbes was lean and muscular, to be sure, but there was a subtle curve to the hip and slenderness in the arms that betrayed her sex. And under the worn denim of her shirt, sweat-dampened in the back, there was a suggestive swell of breasts. Never in her life had Kate seen a woman wear pants. Even the notorious bloomers she'd read about in the newspapers in Boston weren't as scandalous as this.

She continued to stare until she realized that the woman was heading straight toward them, leading a beautiful chestnut mare. She quickly averted her gaze despite the fact that she desperately wanted to see Jessie up close. *This woman will think I have no manners at all, gazing at her like a schoolboy!*

The jangle of spurs grew louder until suddenly the sound stopped and a shadow fell across the wooden sidewalk right in front of her. Kate found herself looking down at the dusty toes of two very well-worn boots. Their owner hitched her horse to the railing and took the two stairs up to the porch in one long stride.

"Howdy, Jessie," John said amiably.

"Afternoon, John," the woman answered as she stepped into the dry goods store.

Kate was surprised at the deep but melodious timbre of her voice. She glanced then at the horse standing quietly before them, taking in the well ridden but still beautiful saddle engraved with an elegantly tooled *JF*. A rifle was tucked into a case on the right side. She turned to John, about to ask if such a remarkable thing as a woman owning property was common on the frontier, but stopped when she heard the spurs behind them again.

"Say, John, you can tell your dad I've got that colt down from the high country if he wants to ride out and see him sometime." Jessie halted on her way out of the store, a box of kitchen supplies under one arm. "Oh, sorry, I didn't mean to be interrupting," she said when she saw that Kate had been about to speak.

Kate looked up into eyes a shade bluer than the clear mountain sky. Her gaze lingered there until she recognized surprise, and then she glanced down from the sun-bleached hair beneath the brim of the cowboy hat over strong cheekbones to a generous mouth and square chin. When she saw the woman color slightly, she looked away, feeling her own face flame. *How rude of me! What has gotten into me!*

"Oh, you're not interrupting, Jessie." John warmed to his role as guide. "This here is Miss Kate Beecher, and she's just come from Boston. Her dad and mine are going to run the paper together now."

Jessie lifted a slim, long-fingered hand, browned from the sun and nicked here and there from the wire she'd been stringing the day before, and quickly removed her hat. She looked down from what seemed to Kate to be a great height and said softly, "I'm pleased to meet you, Miss Beecher. I'm Jessie Forbes. You picked the right time of year to arrive in Montana. Spring and summer are mighty fine seasons." She smiled then, and her eyes flashed a gentle welcome.

Kate smiled back and held out her hand. "I believe it is easily the most beautiful country that I have ever seen, Miss Forbes."

Jessie took her hand in a firm but careful grip and replied, "Please call me Jessie." She held Kate's hand for an instant and then stepped back self-consciously. "Well, John, you give your dad that message. I'd best be getting along."

"Sure, Jessie. See you at the sale."

Though slightly bedazzled, Kate followed the trim line of Jessie's back as she went quickly down the stairs and grasped the reins of her horse. Effortlessly, the rancher swung one long leg over the saddle and regarded Kate almost shyly from her mount.

"Good luck to you, Miss Beecher."

"Thank you, Jessie," she replied, adding quickly, "My name is Kate."

Jessie smiled easily and tipped her hat once again. "Good afternoon, then, Miss Kate. John." With that, she swung her horse away and spurred her into an easy canter out of town.

John didn't seem to notice Kate's quiet concentration as they walked slowly back to the house. As he continued to point out the local sights, Kate nodded absently, all the while reflecting on blue eyes and a fleeting smile, warmer than any she could ever recall.

Oh my, but what would they think of her back in Boston, she thought to herself, unable to forget the odd encounter. She had imagined all manner of new discoveries on the frontier, but she had never dreamed of anything as intriguing as Jessie Forbes. The only women she had met who lived independently, as Jessie did, had been widowed, and even then, they usually lived with family. She did recall two of her teachers, maiden women who shared a brownstone not far from the private school she had attended. They had apparently been friends since their youth and were great companions all their lives. She smiled to herself as she walked along beside John, thinking there was nothing about Jessie Forbes that resembled *those* sedate, proper ladies. She tried to imagine what her mother would make of a woman wearing men's clothing, riding astride a horse, and carrying a gun. No doubt, she would be scandalized.

"You're awfully quiet, Miss Kate," John said. "You're not feeling poorly, are you? We did walk a long ways."

"No, I'm not tired in the least, John," Kate replied kindly. "There's just so much for me to see, and I'm trying to take it all in."

"Well then, you should get back to it."

She took his arm when he shyly offered it, holding her skirts up with the other to avoid the worst of the dust kicked up by passing horses and wagons, while her thoughts returned to a woman with sun-kissed skin and sky blue eyes.

A woman rancher. Yes, what a wonderful new world this is.

CHAPTER THREE

Jessie turned slowly onto her back and gingerly shook each arm and then each leg. *I think I'm all intact, no thanks to anything but good fortune.* Her hat lay several feet away, where it had fallen when she landed on her face.

"Well, you won that round," she muttered good-naturedly as she looked up at the horse standing quietly over her. She got stiffly to her feet, dusted the dirt from her slightly tender backside, and stroked his long, sensitive nose. "How can any horse as friendly as you are be so hard to ride?"

She had acquired the roan stallion in trade several weeks before, and after letting him settle in for a few days, she had saddled him up for the first time. He had accepted the saddle and bridle amiably enough, but Jessie was no sooner seated than he had neatly deposited her on the ground. After the shock had passed, she had laughed heartily, thinking that the rancher who had left with two of her mares might have gotten the better part of the bargain. She would have to remember to invite him to the next big card game so she could even the score.

As the days passed, it became apparent that Rory would indeed be a challenge. He greeted her each time she approached with a friendly shake of his head and nuzzled her shoulder, looking for sugar or apples, but he would not let her ride him.

Finally, that afternoon she had walked him, fully saddled, for almost an hour, and he had been well mannered and obedient. As casually as possible, she had pulled him up and mounted him effortlessly. To her great amazement, he had responded instantly to her touch and walked easily about the corral. When she'd leaned forward to pat his neck and compliment him, just moments ago, he had kicked his hind legs and catapulted her over his head. She was still grumbling to herself over the horse's sly victory when a rumbling voice broke the quiet.

"That was a nice fall you took there, Jess."

She turned to see her foreman leaning against the fence, watching her with just the hint of a smile. Jed Harper was rawboned and weather-beaten, with the ageless face of someone who had lived all his life in the open. He was a good head shorter than her, with ropy muscles and the rolling stride of a man who spent most of his time in the saddle.

"I'm glad it was you saw that and not one of the other men," she said with a rueful grin. "He's a smart one, this Rory."

Had it been anyone other than Jed who had witnessed her most recent defeat, she would have been embarrassed. Jed, however, had been around as long as she could remember, and she had nothing to hide from him. She was no longer certain whether it had been Jed or her father who had taught her to ride, break horses, and shoot a gun.

In the years since her father's death, Jessie had become an able businesswoman and a just boss, but she depended greatly on Jed's common sense and easy way of handling the men who worked on her ranch. She took an active hand in the actual physical running of the ranch, and her presence at roundups, brandings, and auctions was accepted without question. Most of the day-to-day affairs, however, were left to Jed, whom she trusted completely. He, in turn, always let her know he couldn't have been more proud of his own child.

"I've seen them like that before, Jess. Stubborn streak a mile wide. He'll make a great horse if you can win him."

Laughing, Jessie led the stallion toward the barn. "I guess my stubborn streak can stand up to his."

It was cool in the dark outbuilding, and the smell of fresh hay was clean and sweet. Jessie removed the tack and gave Rory a brisk rubdown. There was dirt caked on her face and clothes, and a deep scratch across her right cheek. She would ache later when the bruised muscles stiffened.

Her blond hair was collar length, thick and rich, and she wore it pulled back at her neck with a wide dark ribbon. She was not vain about her physical appearance; in fact, she rarely considered it, and she wore her hair shorter than was fashionable because it was practical. She couldn't very well work with it always in her way.

"I was hoping to bring you into town for the roundup to show you off," she admonished the horse as she worked the dust from his coat with a stiff wire brush. "You'll make a great stud and father fine foals, if you don't turn out to be too wild. People don't want horses they can't ride, you know."

Her voice belied her criticism. She admired his spirit, and she wouldn't break him down if she couldn't eventually tame him with her persistence. "Guess you'll have to sit this one out."

For almost a week every year in the late spring, New Hope was the center of a huge auction where she put her animals up against those of the best ranches in the territory to buy, sell, and trade. It was always an exciting time, and she would be working day and night to purchase animals that would improve her stock and to collect her profits from those she had bred and sold. Doing well at the roundup was a necessity if her ranch was to survive. She, Jed, and most of the hands would drive the horses down early on the first morning for weighing and registering. Then she would be free to look over the other stock being offered and make arrangements with fellow ranchers for sales or stud services.

Jessie had been a part of this process for as long as she could remember. Most of the ranchers had grown used to seeing little Jessie at Tom Forbes's side every year at roundup, and after Tom was killed, it was natural for her to continue. She had earned a reputation as a good breeder and an honest trader. The fact that she was a woman was somehow never an issue, perhaps because she had always been there. Men who wouldn't let their daughters ride astride found nothing unusual in Jessie Forbes riding herd on her own stock or striking a business deal. Jessie was just Jessie.

Straightening up carefully, she grimaced at the ache in her lower back and stretched her long, slender trunk. "Go on, get in there." She slapped the horse's rump. "You can eat now. I'd better get moving, or I'll be too stiff to ride in the morning."

Slowly, she made her way across the yard toward the sprawling wood-and-stone house that had always been her home. Her father had built it to last when he had first staked his claim, well before she was born. It was of simple design, with a kitchen, pantry, parlor, and sitting room downstairs. They had never entertained anyone other than men who came to do business, and the sitting room had become her father's office. This was the room that Jessie preferred.

The heavy leather chairs, gun racks, and shelves of books were strangely restful. A sitting room with lace-covered couches and fine glassware would only have made her nervous. She often read for a few hours at night before the fire in her library, choosing from the collection of books that had been her father's. When she made her semiannual trip into Bannack, the territorial capital, for the supplies she could not get closer to home, she always tried to find a new volume to add.

Her days were full, and she was rarely lonely. On the infrequent evenings when a strange melancholy stole over her, she had only to stand on the porch, looking out on the land that sustained her, and she would find her peace.

"Mr. Schroeder?" Kate asked as her father and his friend joined the women in the parlor following an after-dinner cigar out on the porch. "Please tell us about the roundup tomorrow."

After only a month in New Hope, Kate felt as if she had always lived there. She still had much to learn about everyday life without the comforts that she had been used to, but she viewed each new challenge as a test of her own ability. She looked happy, and she was.

"Humph. Just an excuse for those cowboys to come into town and tear the place up," Hannah grumbled as she reached for her sewing.

Thaddeus laughed. "Don't you go listening to Hannah, now, Kate. The spring roundup is one of the biggest events in this town. Ranchers and drovers come from hundreds of miles, and the place fills up, to be sure. The hotel can't handle 'em all, and the saloon, well…" He glanced at his wife. "I guess things do get a little wild at times, but they're a good-natured bunch."

"Heavens, is it safe to go out?" Martha asked with concern. She pictured hordes of men riding roughshod through the streets.

"Now, Martha," Martin chided, aware that his wife still found the rough western ways unsettling.

"It's not like it used to be, Martha," Thaddeus replied kindly. "The whole town gets involved. There'll be a big celebration the last day of the auction, over at the church. And there's a dance. Most of the women prepare food. My Hannah is known for her pies over the whole territory."

Hannah blushed and shushed him.

"I am so looking forward to it," Kate said with real enthusiasm. This certainly sounded much more interesting than the afternoons she recalled, sitting in a somber parlor discussing topics of no consequence with would-be suitors who didn't appear to care what her thoughts might be. She was relieved to have left that behind, if only temporarily.

"Will all the ranchers be there?" she asked, thinking about one rancher in particular.

As different as the young women of New Hope might be from Kate's friends in Boston, in one way they were very much the same. They still spent their lives learning to be wives. Kate appreciated the way these women toiled so their families might survive in a harsh, unforgiving land, but as she dutifully spent time with Hannah Schroeder learning how to preserve meat without ice or the best way to fashion pillow slips from old dresses, she thought about Jessie Forbes. Jessie owned her own home and went about town doing business unescorted, a daring possibility of which Kate had never even conceived. The quiet, self-possessed rancher was unlike any other woman she had ever met, and Kate wanted to see her again.

"Every rancher in the territory will be here," Thaddeus Schroeder confirmed.

"I'd like to watch the auction tomorrow." Kate looked to her father. "I can, can't I?"

"I gather it's safe enough, isn't it?" Martin asked of Thaddeus, ignoring the concerned expression on his wife's face. He was delighted with how readily Kate had taken to their new home, and although he knew his wife still harbored doubts, he was more certain with each passing day that his decision to bring the family West had been the right one. Why, Kate looked happier than he could ever recall and gave no indication of pining for the luxuries of their previous life. Surely that was proof enough that New Hope was where they belonged. He patted his wife's arm reassuringly. "If she's properly escorted, of course."

Kate wanted to insist that she could manage on her own, but she held her objections. All that mattered now was that she be allowed to go. There would be time enough to convince her parents that she did not require an escort simply to walk through town.

Thaddeus nodded. "Why of course. I'll have John Emory take Kate over in the morning to see where the stock will be corralled. Some of the nearby ranchers will be here by then."

Ranchers. The ranchers will be coming into town tomorrow. Kate smiled demurely, while inside she seethed with excitement. "Thank you. That will be just perfect."

❖

John Schroeder had seen traveling photographers before, and his father had several examples of their craft hanging in the newspaper office, but he had never seen a photograph made. He had also never seen a woman do anything of the kind.

"Father didn't say you'd be wanting to tote half the house out here with us," he grumbled, but in good humor. He grunted slightly as he shifted the heavy cases he carried in both hands.

"Oh John!" Kate laughed and looked up at him fondly. "How could I miss this opportunity to make photographs?"

"Are you sure about all this?" he asked. In one of the cases he could hear liquid sloshing.

Secretly, he was astonished that Kate could make those pictures he had seen at the Beecher house. She had tried to explain the process to him, saying it was quite simple, but he could not grasp it. The mystery of it only served to elevate her in his eyes.

"Don't worry," she assured him. "This was my father's equipment, and I've helped him make photographs since I was a little girl. He grew tired of it, but I never have. It was the *one* thing I would not leave behind." She looked around her at the sharply rising hills and the expanse of endless sky and thought that she had never seen country more beautiful. "I can't wait to capture just a little of this on the plates."

"Humph. Just a roundup, like all the others," he complained, but his voice was light-hearted.

People greeted them with friendly hellos as they passed by. It was a common sight to see him escorting the pretty Beecher girl about town, and John thought himself the most fortunate man in town when he did so. He would gladly have carried the damn cases all day.

"Say, why don't we go over under those trees," he suggested. "You can see the auction stand and the corrals across the yard."

Kate nodded her approval. Already, she was amazed at the number of people filling the street. There was a contagious excitement in the air, borne on the sounds of men shouting and agitated livestock snorting and whinnying. She was captivated by the sight of the large animals milling about in the pens, huge masses of restless power. The immediacy and urgency of life in this untamed place was thrilling.

The cowboys who tended the corrals leaned up against fences or trees, talking quietly in groups, sharing a smoke. They certainly didn't look wild to Kate, as Hannah's ominous recounts had led her to expect. The dusty trail hand did not hold her interest, however. She scanned the crowd, looking for Jessie Forbes's distinctive figure, but was disappointed not to find the rancher among the early arrivals.

Contenting herself with photographing the surrounding activity, she was soon lost in her work. She exposed several plates, intent on depicting the quiet anticipation of the waiting crowd before the auction began. It was a time-consuming process because she had to fix the wet plates almost immediately or the surface would dry and lose the image she had so carefully sought. She was in the process of exposing her last plate when she heard John at her elbow.

"Miss Kate, you'd better let me get that contraption out of here," he said urgently. "There's a herd coming this way, and you're going to be mighty close."

"Just fifteen more seconds, John," Kate answered calmly. This was a good exposure, perhaps the best that morning, and she was not going to ruin it. It had taken her nearly an hour to prepare the mixture of egg precipitate and chemicals that coated the plates and longer still to develop each one into a finished photograph. She could not afford to waste a plate or worse, lose an image, by rushing.

"Please, Miss Kate!" John shouted, tugging at her sleeve.

Under the camera cloth, Kate heard muffled shouts to her right and felt her camera support tremble. Even as the sound of thundering hoofbeats grew closer, she couldn't imagine what the fuss was about.

"Three, two, one..." she whispered, closing the shutter and lifting the cloth from her shoulders. "Oh!" she cried, grasping John's arm in stunned alarm.

Not twenty feet away, a solid wall of horses streamed into an open pen as a dozen cowboys galloped back and forth along the edge of the herd, trying to direct the fast moving animals into the corrals. Men surrounded her, shouting and waving their hats. A haze of dust billowed upward, engulfing her, and Kate stumbled backward to the shelter of the trees, coughing and wiping dirt from her eyes. John had the presence of mind to drag her camera back with him as he rushed to join her. He shouted something to her, but his words were lost in the uproar of bellowing men and rampaging horses.

Through eyes streaming with tears, Kate watched the cowboys herd the stragglers into the pen. The leader of the group leaned down from his saddle to swing the corral gate shut. Then, with a quick flick of the horse's head and a swift jab of his heels to the huge animal's flanks, he spurred his mount directly toward Kate and John.

Anxiously, Kate edged a little closer to the boy as the horse and rider drew down upon them, kicking up clouds of dirt anew. She was sure that they were about to be trampled. When the charging horse was only a few feet away, or so it seemed to Kate, she saw the rider rise up out of the seat and dismount on the run. Before she could catch her breath, the cowboy, caked in dirt from head to toe, grabbed John by the shirtfront.

"Damn it, John! What's got into you, letting her get that close to the pens! If a stray had got loose from that bunch, it could have run her down. I've a good mind to throw you into that corral over there and let my horses stomp some sense into you!"

Jessie Forbes was so mad she couldn't see straight. Her heart was still pounding with the sudden surge of panic she had experienced upon spying Kate standing right in her path as she led her herd down the main street into town. The horses in the lead had already begun to spread out across the entire width of the thoroughfare, and Jessie had barely had time to direct the wranglers between Kate and the galloping steeds. Another minute and Kate would have been under their hooves.

It was only because she liked John Schroeder that she didn't do more damage than shaking him. She forced herself to let him go, turning to ask Kate, "Are you all right, Miss Beecher?"

Kate stared open-mouthed, more surprised by Jessie's sudden appearance than the previous threat of unbridled charging horses. The rancher's face was streaked with dirt, and there was an angry welt running across her right cheek. Her shirt was plastered to her chest with sweat. She stood with her hands curled around the belt of her wide, black holster, her long legs planted a little apart. Her hands trembled slightly as they clenched the leather, and Kate had the momentary urge to hold one of those strong, capable-looking hands while assuring the obviously worried woman that she was unharmed. Then she took in the angry countenance and felt the need to defend her young escort.

"It wasn't his fault," Kate croaked, her throat parched and sore from the dust.

Finally remembering to sweep off her hat, Jessie forced a smile through her anger. "Now that's where you're wrong, Miss Beecher. It *is* right well his fault. He should have looked after you, being a newcomer. He knows what to expect around here on roundup day."

John nodded his head abashedly, having forgotten his initial scare when Jessie had grabbed him. He'd thought for a minute there that he was in for a whupping and suspected he probably deserved one. "You're right, Jessie. She could have gotten—"

"Now just one minute," Kate interrupted hotly, her dark eyes blazing. "I am not a helpless child, you know. I have two legs, and I could have moved if I had wanted! I certainly do not need either one of you deciding where I should stand."

Jessie and John stared at her wordlessly, and Kate stared back, her face flushed. She saw a grin begin to flicker across Jessie's fine mouth, and her anger slowly ebbed. Then Jessie tilted her head back and laughed, and, after a second, Kate joined her. John gaped at them as if they had both taken leave of their senses.

Jessie's tense body relaxed, and she smiled down at Kate. "What was that thing you had out there anyhow?"

"A camera. I was trying to capture the feeling of this whole thing," Kate answered, taking in the street and the corrals with a sweep of her arm.

"Well, you almost got more of a *feel* for it than you bargained on, Miss Beecher."

"Kate," Kate said softly.

Jessie's eyes sparkled. "Kate."

"You've hurt yourself," Kate said, studying Jessie with a worried expression.

"What?" Jessie replied, confused. When Kate's soft hand brushed gently across her swollen cheek, Jessie blushed and turned her head away. "Oh, that's nothing. I've been having a running battle with a new stallion I've had the misfortune of acquiring. He and I don't see eye to eye on which one of us is the boss just yet."

"I find that hard to believe," Kate answered steadily, her eyes fixed on the rancher's face. Jessie impressed her as being the most capable woman she could imagine.

Jessie wasn't sure why Kate's words stirred a flutter in her chest, but she cleared her throat and addressed John firmly. "I've got to see to my horses, John. You make sure you take care of Kate, now."

"I will," John mumbled contritely.

Kate placed her hand lightly on Jessie's sleeve and said boldly, "Would you show me your animals later?"

Jessie tensed. Damn if her arm didn't shake where Kate touched her. "Well, they're just horses, you know. Nothing special."

"They're amazing," Kate insisted. She *did* want to know more about the roundup, but mostly, she wanted an excuse to spend more time with this tough but strangely gentle woman. She found Jessie's concern for her well-being touching, even though she knew herself quite able to look after her own welfare. "I'd really like to see them."

"All right, then," Jessie relented, surprised by Kate's request. It wasn't the sort of thing to which most well-bred young ladies took a liking. Kate Beecher, on the other hand, didn't strike her as being the pampered sort—not when she'd been standing out in the midst of a near stampede, as calm as could be. "I'll be busy most of the morning with the weighing. If you're here this afternoon, I'll be happy to show you."

Kate smiled softly. "I'll be here."

With a tip of her hat, Jessie mounted and galloped back to the corral, calling to her men as she rode. Kate watched the wranglers fall in around her, thinking she made quite the most dashing figure of a cowboy.

CHAPTER FOUR

Jessie worked steadily the rest of the morning in a makeshift shed by the auction stands, registering her stock and seeing to the hands. As she paid her men their wages, she knew full well that they'd likely spend a large share of it during the next week. Most of them would come straggling back to the ranch when their money was gone, ready to sign on for another year. A few would answer the call of wanderlust, eager to discover what was over the next mountain ridge. Most who left town would never pass this way again.

Life on the frontier was a hard one, and she didn't begrudge her men their pleasures. She enjoyed a good hand of cards herself and more often than not came away a winner. It was no secret that the saloon offered more than gaming tables and good whiskey, too. Everyone in town knew that the "good-time" women who lived upstairs in the hotel earned their keep by befriending the cowboys who passed through. Jessie figured those women were only doing what they had to do to survive, and she accepted that as uncritically as her men accepted her.

"Don't spend it all tonight, Sam," she said as she handed the draft to her lead trail man.

"No, ma'am," he exclaimed, looking a little sheepish.

"You make sure the boys don't cause trouble this week. I don't want it said the Forbes boys were running wild."

"I'll see to it, Miss Jessie," the big man replied earnestly. There were some transients among their group, but most of the hands had been with Jessie through more than one roundup, and all of them were proud to work for her. She was fair and paid top wages. Her ability to rope and ride with the best of them had earned her their respect and loyalty.

Jessie pushed her chair back from the rickety wooden table and gathered her account papers. "You can tell the boys the week is theirs, but I expect you all to ride out of here with me come next Monday,"

"They'll be pleased to hear that, ma'am." Sam grinned at her. "It's been a long time between roundups."

"I know it, Sam." Jessie ran a weary hand over her face. "But we've a fine herd to show for it, and I'm right pleased with all of you."

Sam flushed, happy with the compliment. He tipped his hat and turned to leave, almost bumping into Kate. "Sorry, miss," he said as he walked away.

"Am I early?" Kate asked as she approached the table, smiling.

"No, I've just finished," Jessie said, smiling back. She folded her papers and slipped them into the saddlebag by her side. Standing, she rubbed her face again ruefully. "If you'll give me a bit, though, I need to get washed up. I feel like one of my horses just now—rode hard and put up wet."

For an instant, Kate struggled for the meaning of the expression, but a closer look at Jessie told the story. She was still dusty from the trail, and there were circles shadowing her dark blue eyes. She was clearly exhausted.

"How long has it been since you've slept in a bed?" Kate asked.

Jessie shrugged. "It takes the better part of a month to get the herd down from the high country where they winter, then foal in the spring. Always stragglers getting lost up some canyon or other. I need every able body on the ranch to bring them in. Not many of us slept more than a few hours in a row for a while."

"We could do this another time," Kate offered, trying to hide her disappointment. She had hurried through dinner preparations with her mother so that she might have the rest of the day free to spend with Jessie.

"Oh, no." Jessie laughed. "No way am I going to be tucked abed somewhere when I could be making a deal, or," she finished shyly, "taking a walk for no other reason than the fun of it."

Kate blushed, unaccountably pleased. "Are you staying at the hotel, then?"

"Yes. Most everybody's got a room there for the week," Jessie said as they turned toward town. She glanced at the sky, aware for the first time what an unusually fine day it was. She couldn't recall a prettier day, but then she rarely took the time to admire one. "I won't be long. Where do you want me to meet you?"

"I'll walk you to the hotel, if you don't mind," Kate replied, suddenly afraid that Jessie might change her mind after all.

"I'd enjoy the company," Jessie said quietly, surprised that it was true. She was used to going long stretches without talking to anyone, except maybe Jed about some problem at the ranch. The idea of walking in the warm afternoon sun with Kate Beecher seemed more than pleasant. "You folks all settled?"

"I'm not sure that I'd call it 'settled,' exactly," Kate said with a laugh as they strolled through the town toward the hotel, which, judging by the hordes of people milling in the street and crowding the board sidewalks nearby, was clearly the center of activity. "My father is quite beside himself with pleasure, but it's hard for my mother. The simple things we took for granted, like household items and ready-made clothes, are rarities here. Hannah Schroeder has been a great help, and I think I'm beginning to master the basics, but it's much different than I expected."

Jessie had never given such things much thought. Life at the ranch was simple. What they couldn't buy in the way of tools or goods, they made or went without. She didn't need more than the clothes she worked in. Game was plentiful on the range, and enough of her neighbors farmed that she could buy food staples for herself and her men locally. "I imagine it feels pretty uncivilized out here to you," she mused.

"No," Kate replied quietly. "It feels free."

Jessie heard the wistful tone in Kate's voice and tried to envision another life, a life where she wasn't free to come and go as she pleased, where she wasn't free to make her own choices. She couldn't imagine it.

"Well, the work never ends, but at the end of the day, you know you owe nothing to no man for what you've built. I guess that's what brings a lot of folks out here," Jessie said. "And why so many stay even when it seems foolish."

"Foolish?" Kate's tone was incredulous. "Oh, no, not that. Brave is what I'd call it. Brave and admirable."

Jessie felt a flush of pride, as if she'd done something worthwhile just because this young woman thought so. *Now that's foolish.* But she enjoyed the sensation anyhow.

They walked in companionable silence the remaining distance to the hotel. Closer now, Kate saw cowboys in groups and pairs straggle in and out of the saloon on the first floor, shouting to friends they had apparently not seen for months. Many waved or called to Jessie, who greeted most by name. Piano music floated through the open doors, providing a festive background to the general cacophony. She started toward the swinging doors, but Jessie caught her hand.

"There's a stairway around back here," Jessie said, leading the way down the narrow alley between the hotel and the land office. "That's no place for you in there."

"And you?" Kate questioned, amused at Jessie's protective attitude but warmed by it, too.

"Oh, that's different. I've ridden with most of those men and played cards with more than a few. Had to carry a couple of 'em home on more than one occasion. But no lady would want to go in there. Roundup time is a little crazy."

"I see," Kate said gravely.

Jessie caught the faint mocking tone in Kate's voice and saw the shadow of a smile flicker across her smooth features. "Sorry. Don't mean to be preaching at you."

"I'm teasing you." Kate laughed and squeezed Jessie's hand before letting go. "Come on, let's get you upstairs."

They climbed the outside wooden steps to the second floor and walked down a narrow hallway with a half dozen doors on each side until they reached Jessie's room. A plain iron bedstead held a narrow mattress, a single bureau stood against one wall with a pitcher and basin on the top, and a threadbare braid rug covered part of the floor. Jessie drew the only chair up to the window so Kate would have a good view of the activities below.

"I'll just be a minute. I want to wash the dust off my face and get into some pants that don't stand up by themselves."

"You don't need to hurry." Kate watched as Jessie unbuckled the heavy gun strapped to her thigh and laid it casually on the bed before stripping off the leather chaps she wore over her pants. "Is that what you call a six-shooter?"

Jessie looked over at her, poised with one foot up to pull off her boots. "Most sidearms nowadays hold six bullets in the chamber. They vary a bit depending on the caliber of the bullets. That's a Colt forty-five. All the Army carries them. They call it a peacemaker, but I suspect they're foolin' about that."

"Oh, I see," Kate said, noting the sarcasm in the way Jessie said Army. "I take it you don't care for soldiers."

"I don't know as how I like or dislike 'em, really. It just gets a bit aggravating when the government sends troops who don't understand the land or the customs or the people, and then tries to say they're the law."

"Have they bothered you at the ranch?" Kate asked, genuinely curious. It had never occurred to her before that people like Jessie, whose families had carved a life out of this inhospitable land, often at great sacrifice, might not welcome the representatives of a government far removed.

"They help themselves to a cow now or then," Jessie allowed. "I'd gladly give them what they want when they need food, but they don't seem to think asking is necessary."

"That probably never occurred to them," Kate remarked, outraged on Jessie's behalf.

"I imagine we do a lot of things different out here than back East," Jessie said.

"Have you ever been to the East?" Kate turned her chair from the window, finding nothing in the streets below that interested her as much as Jessie Forbes.

Jessie poured a basin of water as she responded. "My father said my mother would have wanted me to go for more schooling." She splashed her face, then doused her head and reached blindly for a towel. After she'd dried off her face, she remarked, "I hated the idea, but I was supposed to go when I was seventeen. My father was stubborn on that point."

"But you didn't?" Kate asked with interest.

Jessie stiffened slightly as she opened the valise at the end of the bed. Pulling clean but faded denim pants and an embroidered shirt from the case, she answered softly, "My father died in a stampede a month before I was supposed to go. I had to stay and run the ranch."

"Oh, I'm sorry, Jessie." Hearing the edge of sorrow in Jessie's voice, Kate instantly regretted bringing up the painful memory.

"It's all right. That sort of thing happens out here."

Kate said nothing. She couldn't imagine losing her father so tragically, and she knew how much it must have hurt. She didn't think Jessie could be that much older than her, and she marveled at her composure, thinking that she had rarely met anyone more self-assured.

Still sorting her thoughts, Kate was caught off guard as Jessie slipped off her grimy shirt and pants. Involuntarily, she drew in a sharp breath, surprised by the thin cotton undershirt the other woman wore in place of a corset and alarmed by the large bruise covering her left thigh. "You *are* hurt!"

Jessie stopped in the midst of stepping into her clean pants, surprised by Kate's outburst. She saw the direction of Kate's gaze and looked down. "Oh, that. Pretty sorry excuse for a rancher, huh?" Chuckling, she pulled up her pants and tucked in her shirt. "Just another little present from that stallion of mine."

"He's obviously a handful if he got the best of you." Kate watched the easy way Jessie moved, admiring her supple strength. Her limbs were slender, but every action was accompanied by a tightening of the muscles beneath her smooth skin. So different from her own softer shape. When her stomach suddenly fluttered, accompanied by a strange tripping of her pulse, Kate averted her gaze in confusion.

"You must find this town a great disappointment after Boston," Jessie said, unaware of Kate's discomfort.

"Oh no, I love it!" Kate was startled to realize just how true that was. "Life is so different here…so much more exciting. There is so much to learn, and besides, there is no one like you in Boston…" She blushed suddenly, embarrassed by her forward remark.

Jessie laughed and reached for her holster. "I don't imagine I'd fit in too well back there."

"No," Kate said softly. "No, you wouldn't."

Jessie was caught by the quiet intensity in her voice. Kate seemed quite unlike the shy young women Jessie had grown up with in New Hope. Despite Kate's sophistication, she was easy to talk to, and her enthusiasm was contagious. Jessie was enjoying their conversation more than she'd expected. With a grin, she pulled on her worn leather boots and said, "I suppose it will take some getting used to, but I hope you'll be happy here, Kate."

"I feel as if this is where I belong," Kate answered, never meaning it more than she did in that moment.

Jessie felt wonderful all of a sudden. Her fatigue had magically vanished. "Do you still want to see those horses of mine?"

"Oh, yes!"

"Come on, then." Jessie crossed the room and took Kate's hand gently. "We'd better go before it gets to be dinnertime."

Kate was stunned by Jessie's careful strength and the utter tenderness of her touch. Quite unable to move, she sat staring up at Jessie, whose eyes suddenly grew dark. A pulse beat visibly in her neck, just above the collar of her shirt. Kate felt her own heart beat hard against the inside of her chest. For a moment, neither of them spoke. Kate swallowed, aware of the faint tremor in Jessie's fingers. Hers were shaking too.

"Yes," Kate whispered as they both drew shyly away at the same time. She rose, trying to ignore the slight unsteadiness in her limbs. "We should go."

Kate and Jessie traveled first to the auction pens. Jessie's herd was one of the largest, and also one of the most interesting to Kate's artistic eye. No two of the sturdy horses were alike—some were white with pale rust spots, others solid dark, and still others multishaded, much like a patchwork quilt.

"They're so beautiful!" Kate leaned eagerly over the chest-high, split-rail fence for a better look as the animals circled within the confines of the corral. "I've never seen such patterns before."

"Our stock is almost pure Appaloosa—Plains Indian bred—with a little wild mustang thrown in to make 'em tough," Jessie proclaimed proudly. "My father was one of the first ranchers in this area. He was on his way to the Oregon territory with all the other fools looking for gold when my mother convinced him that land was where the real value lay, or so he told it."

"So they settled here?"

"After a spell." Jessie leaned a foot up on the rail and dangled her forearms over the top of the corral, watching one particularly frisky colt kick up his heels. "Back then, the Indians and the settlers still got along pretty well. The Indians bartered their horses for supplies that the expeditions brought. My father found himself a couple of hands as crazy as him, and he started chasing down the wild horses to build our line. As long as he stayed clear of the Indian hunting grounds, there wasn't any problem." She frowned. "All the problems started with the damn Army telling the Indians where they had to live." She looked quickly at Kate. "Sorry for the cussing."

"I won't faint from a word, Jessie." She had heard of the "Indian troubles," but it had seemed very much like the war with the South—something that didn't really affect her. Suddenly, it seemed much more important. "Is there fighting around here?"

"Not yet," Jessie said, her expression darkening. "But with more and more settlers coming all the time, moving farther into Indian land, I don't know…"

"The Indians we saw on the trail seemed friendly. Shy, mostly."

"Seems as if there ought to be enough room out here for everybody." Jessie smiled and touched Kate's hand lightly. "Come on, let's walk some more, and I'll show you where the auction will be."

Kate was filled with questions, one tumbling out after the other, and Jessie answered good-naturedly as they strolled from corral to corral or rested beneath the shade trees when the heat became too much. They didn't notice the sun starting to set until a brisk breeze caused Kate to shiver slightly and pull her crocheted shawl tightly around her shoulders.

"Lord, Kate. It's later than I thought." Looking up at the sky, Jessie was amazed that she had lost track of time. That was something she never did. "You should be getting back."

"Oh no! There's so much more I want to know. Plus," she added impulsively, "I'm having too much fun."

Jessie laughed, twirling her hat between her long, graceful fingers. "So am I, but won't your parents worry?"

"Probably." Kate sighed. "Despite the fact that I'm eighteen and quite capable of looking after myself."

"I expect you are," Jessie said seriously. "But this isn't Boston. Young women can't be out wandering after dark. I'll take you home."

"And I suppose you're quite safe?" Kate retorted. "I'm not a child, and I'm quite as capable as you. Why is it that you can walk about and I can't?"

The sudden storm threatening in Kate's eyes brought Jessie to a halt. "Kate," she said softly, "I'm not like you. There isn't a man in this town who would try to take advantage of me."

Kate blushed, understanding her meaning and feeling foolish for not realizing that Jessie had only been thinking of her safety. It had nothing to do with her age and much more to do with the gun on Jessie's thigh.

"I'm sorry," she said swiftly.

Jessie shook her head. "No need. Now, let's get you home. Where is it?"

"At the other end of town, near the south fork."

The day was fading as they walked, the last golden rays slanting over the rough boards and irregular angles of the buildings, bathing the town in a warm glow. The mountains, capped by a deep purple and deep pink sky, created a backdrop more beautiful than any painting Kate had ever seen. Townspeople making their way home and cowboys lounging on the sidewalks nodded as they passed. With Jessie striding confidently beside her, Kate realized that she had never felt so free, and yet so secure. She wanted to take Jessie's arm as she often took John Emory's when they were out, but something held her back. Jessie was quite unlike anyone she had ever met—and Kate was very aware that she felt far different walking with Jessie than she ever had with John. She'd never passed such happy hours with anyone before, not even her father.

As they approached the gate in front of Kate's home, Jessie stopped. "I'll say good night now, Kate."

"Come in for dinner. Please." Kate placed her hand on Jessie's arm. The day had been too wonderful for it to end, and being with Jessie was what had made it special. Jessie made not just the town, but the whole countryside, come alive for Kate with her stories of her family and the other settlers. And even more, she'd made Kate feel as if no question was too foolish to answer. "It's the least I can do after you walked all this way."

Jessie looked away, uncomfortable. "No, thank you. I've got to check on the stock anyhow. You go on in."

Kate tried not to show her disappointment as she squeezed Jessie's forearm briefly. "I had a wonderful time, Jessie. Thank you."

Jessie smiled, her eyes meeting Kate's. "No need to thank me for something I enjoyed more than anything I can recall in a long time."

Reluctantly, Kate made her way to the porch, but she stood for long minutes leaning on the railing, watching Jessie's retreating form blend into the night.

Chapter Five

K ate!" Martha rose from her chair in the living room, setting her sewing aside as Kate came hurriedly through the door. "Where have you been? It's late and we were worried sick." She grabbed her by the shoulders and peered at her intently. "I was about to send your father out to search for you."

"For heaven's sake, Martha," Martin exclaimed. "Let the girl talk!"

"I was down at the auction grounds. You knew that," Kate answered, her thoughts still on her afternoon with Jessie. "And it's not even dark yet."

"I know I've said this is a safe town, but this week especially, it's not safe for a young girl out alone at this hour," Martin said.

"I was *not* alone," Kate replied, more forcefully than she had intended. Only moments ago, she had experienced an independence she'd never imagined, simply spending an afternoon as she chose, walking with a woman she admired. Now her parents acted as if she weren't capable of basic good judgment. Rankled by their well-meaning restraints, she pointed out, "I was with a friend and quite safe."

"And who *was* that young man who brought you home?" Martha queried archly.

Kate flushed a hot, deep scarlet. For a moment, she was too angry to speak. Then she asserted indignantly, "That was *not* a young man. That was Jessie Forbes. She's a rancher from north of town."

"A woman!" Martha declared, appalled.

Uncertain why she did, Kate felt instantly protective of Jessie. *Silly,* she thought, *because if anyone doesn't need protecting, it's Jessie Forbes.* Still, she faced her mother with a defiant tilt to her chin, her black eyes flashing against her pale skin.

Martin chuckled. "Kate couldn't have been with anyone safer, my dear. Jessie Forbes is an extremely capable young woman. I met her at the newspaper office some weeks ago. As Kate said, she runs a ranch—apparently quite successfully. She's bright and has a sound head on her shoulders."

Martha turned from daughter to husband, a shocked expression on her face. "I saw this young woman, Martin, and it's a…a…a *disgrace.* She was wearing pants!"

"Well goodness, Martha. This isn't Boston. You could hardly expect her to tend her herd in a dress," he replied easily. "Out here women are compelled to be more practical."

"Practical!" Martha, who even now would not consider wearing the popular bloomer, was outraged. "I hope this isn't the kind of thing that you find admirable. No decent woman would be found dressed like that in public. And I do believe she was wearing a gun!"

"Actually, it's a Colt forty-five peacemaker, Mother," Kate announced with a rebellious edge to her voice. She dropped her shawl on a chair and walked to her father. She took his arm, avoiding her mother's astounded stare. "Shall we have dinner?"

Jessie checked her stock, and once assured that they'd been bedded down safely, returned to her hotel room. After slinging her holster over the chair back, she kicked off her boots and stretched out on the bed, meaning only to close her eyes for a moment. She thought back to the afternoon and the pleasure she had drawn from Kate's company. With the memory of Kate's quick smile playing through her mind, she drifted off to sleep to dream of laughing dark eyes and a gentle hand on her arm.

When she awakened shortly after nine that night, she was ravenous. In the mood for a thick steak and some fried potatoes, she washed quickly, threw on a leather vest over her shirt, and went in search of food in the nearly deserted hotel dining room. She ate alone and then ambled into the saloon. The din of male voices was considerable, and the air was ripe with the odor of horses, well-worked men, and rivers of whiskey. She pushed her way through the crowd to the end of the bar, away from the bulk of the cowboys and the occasional dance-hall girl.

"Evening, Frank. Guess business is good, huh?" she greeted the bartender.

"Jessie Forbes!" shouted the portly, bewhiskered man behind the long, scarred bar. "Good to see you. Yep, there's quite a crowd here tonight. Can I get you something?"

"I think a brandy," she replied, fishing a coin from her denim pants.

Drink in hand, she turned to watch the room, tipping her glass in greeting now and then when someone called to her. Those who didn't know her personally had heard of her from others. She did not feel strange in the room full of men, because, in many ways, she was like them. She lived and worked on the same land as they, sweated the same on a hard day's ride, and bled just as easily when a horse kicked a stone her way or a jerked rope burned a raw gash across her palm. She gave it no more thought than she did to what the next day would bring. She was a rancher; that was her life.

A man edged close to her in the press of bodies that grew steadily denser near the bar as the night wore on. "Cards, Jess?"

"Hank Trilby," she said with pleasure. "How are you? And how are things at your ranch?"

"I brought my first herd down today, Jess, and it's a fine bunch." The tall, dark-haired cowboy grinned with pride. "Hope you take a look at them tomorrow."

Hank had been with her father before his death and had stayed on for a year or two after Jessie took over the ranch. When he had a chance to buy into a spread nearby, Jessie had willingly backed him. She had not been wrong. Hank owned the ranch now.

"I'll do that, Hank. I've been looking for a few new mares." She signaled the barman for a refill. "Did I hear you say cards?"

Hank laughed, pointing to a table at one side of the room where four men sat dealing cards. "We've been waiting for an easy mark," he teased.

Jessie laughed. "Haven't you got enough there already?"

Well after midnight, Jessie pushed her chair back and tossed her cards down. "That's it, boys. If I stay any longer, I'll be selling next year's herd."

Several men laughed, knowing that, if anything, she was slightly ahead. As she rose from the table, a soft voice at her elbow murmured, "Hello, Montana."

Jessie's gaze fell on a woman who was nearly her height and barely a handful of years older. She was voluptuous where Jessie was lean, and her long blond hair cascaded thickly over bare, milk-pale shoulders. Her emerald green silk dress was low cut and close fitting, with a constraining bodice that boldly lifted her breasts to the verge of immodesty and beyond. Her hazel eyes looked weary.

"Why, hello, Mae," Jessie replied warmly. "I was about ready to turn in, but I'd be pleased if you'd join me for a brandy first. You can catch me up on all the news."

Mae gave a deep-throated chuckle and rested her well-kept hand against Jessie's sturdy shoulder. "*You* can have a brandy, Montana. I'll have a whiskey, thanks."

Jessie smiled and made a path for them to the bar. As she placed Mae's drink down, she recalled the first time they had met. It must have been her first roundup after her father had died. She had been barely eighteen and had come looking for Jed in the saloon one night when their best brood mare had gone down with colic out in the stockyard.

The saloon had been more crowded than ever. As she'd searched the room for her men, a big, burly Texan, a stranger, grabbed her roughly from behind.

"Now looky here, will you, boys? Just take a gander at what wandered in. Isn't she a fine one, though, and wearing a sidearm, too!" He had laughed drunkenly and pulled her hat off, one hand under her chin, the other still grasping her arm.

Out of the corner of her eye, Jessie saw Jed with several others heading toward her, blood in their eyes. In a minute, there would be a brawling fight, or worse. She stood very still and raised one hand slightly, waving her men away. Jed stopped, his body tense, and signaled to the others to wait, but his eyes never left Jessie's face.

Pulling her hat from the Texan's grasp, she'd stepped back, freeing her other arm as she did so. Slowly, with careful deliberation, she replaced her hat and regarded the leering cowboy.

"I'm Jessie Forbes. You must be new around here or else you'd know that. I don't believe I know your name. I'm here looking for my men, and I'd appreciate it if you'd let me through." She'd spoken quietly, but her words carried to those nearest her. Several men turned a watchful eye on the cowboy. The air crackled with tension.

"Oh, you'd like to get by, would you?" he mocked, swaying slightly and making another grab for her. "How would you like to come upstairs with me instead? Might be I could show you a good time."

Jessie sidestepped quickly and remained facing him. "Mister, I wouldn't take any pleasure in killing you, but you're wearing out my patience. These fellas here are all trying to enjoy this roundup, and so am I. Nobody wants trouble. Now, I don't want to have my men get all busted up trying to make you be reasonable, so if you don't go off somewhere and let me be, I'm gonna have to shoot you myself." She hadn't made any move toward her gun, but several cowboys nearby drew sharp breaths and moved out of the way.

The stranger laughed hoarsely, his eyes flickering to the faces around him. None were friendly. "You think you can take me?" he jeered, licking his lips, which were suddenly dry.

"I can, but I'd rather not." Her voice was soft, but every man in the room heard her.

He looked at the deadly calm in her eyes and dropped his gaze. "I ain't never shot no woman, and you ain't gonna be the first," he muttered, backing slowly away.

As quickly as it had begun, it was over, but Jessie had won her rightful place in the mind of every man present. As she'd made her way through the crowd, a woman approached, stopping her with a hand on her arm. Her eyes had been as green as spring grass, deep and warm.

"I want to thank you for keeping these damn fools from tearing up this place. I'm afraid some of my girls would have been hurt. Mind you, I think you're daft."

That had happened six roundups ago, and over the years since, she and Mae had become friends. Whenever Jessie was in town, she made it a point to stop in the saloon to say hello or buy Mae a drink after the last of the cowhands had staggered off at the end of the night.

Their friendship was an unconscious appreciation between two women who were often misunderstood, and Jessie had learned to value their moments together. She could talk to Mae in a way that she could to no one else, not even Jed.

"Hey, Montana, what are you dreaming about?" Mae asked as she circled her glass over the top of the bar, watching the dark liquid swirl close to the brim.

Jessie smiled at the woman pressed close against her side and leaned nearer still to make herself heard. "I was remembering that first night when I met you."

"Oh Lord, that was a sight." Mae laughed, downing the whiskey shot in one practiced flick of her wrist. "You and that cowboy in a standoff. Would you have really shot that fella?"

Jessie grinned suddenly. "I don't know. I hadn't thought about it yet." She laughed at the look of dismay on her companion's face. "How are you, Mae? It seems like an age since we've talked."

"Oh, a little older, Jess, but still holding up. Haven't seen you around too much these last few months. Not forgetting old friends, are you?" Mae searched Jessie's face, realizing once again how fine looking she was. *Too handsome for a woman, but too pleasing to the eye for a man.*

Jessie smiled at her fondly and shook her head. "Not you, Mae. I couldn't forget you."

Mae colored slightly and gazed at their reflections in the mirror behind the bar, choosing her words carefully. "Say, Montana, who was that young woman I saw you strolling through town with today? Don't think I know her."

Jessie turned startled eyes on Mae. "Why, her name is Kate Beecher. She and her family just moved here from Boston. I didn't see you. Why didn't you call out?"

"Oh! I was busy doing something, as I recollect. An Easterner, you say?" She sounded wary.

"What's the matter?" Jessie asked, surprised by the suspicion in her voice.

Mae forced a laugh and looked up at Jessie, saying lightly, "Why nothing, Jess. It's just that you have to remember those Easterners are flighty. They come out here and everything is new and different, and they fall in love with the sparkle of it. Only, after a while, they get tired of it and throw it all away like a worn-out shoe."

"Kate's not like that," Jessie said with certainty.

"Well, not now maybe, but let's see what one hard winter does to all that bright-eyed wonder."

"Some folks aren't meant for this life, I'll give you that. But Kate…" Jessie smiled at the memory of Kate's enthusiasm and endless questions. "She's not like some of these ladies who won't cross the road if it's raining lest their shoes get muddy. She's got more to her than that."

Mae watched the light play in Jess's eyes, recognizing the spark she'd never seen there before for what it was, and knew her cautions would fall on deaf ears. But she pressed on, because Jess's heart was too tender to leave unguarded. "Just remember that what you feel ain't always the same as what somebody else feels."

Jessie frowned at Mae, struggling to understand what she was talking about. She was still thinking about it later that night when she fell tiredly into bed.

Chapter Six

K ate was at the auction as early as she could manage the next morning, having recruited John Emory to carry her camera and equipment once again. This time she chose a spot that wasn't directly in the path of careening livestock.

Other women from town had set up tables under a grove of trees just beyond the stockyards and were providing refreshments and sandwiches to the men congregating in front of the stands. Children raced about while worried mothers followed frantically behind them. And the ranchers and cowboys kept coming, driving herds into town twenty-four hours a day. Their numbers had swelled during the night, and the sound of boisterous revelry had filled the streets well after midnight.

Kate had lain awake for hours, listening to the echoes of laughter on the night air, thinking about the day she'd had. She could not recall a time that she had ever enjoyed more. She could have talked with Jessie Forbes for hours, and she so wanted the chance to see her again. When she had announced at breakfast that she was planning on returning to the auction, her mother had objected.

"What could possibly interest you in that place?" Martha asked in exasperation. "Nothing but dirt, animals, and rough men."

"Everything," Kate had excitedly replied. "There is so much to see, and so many things to learn."

"And what about your plans to help Hannah with the spinning today?"

Kate knew that her mother considered this, at least, a useful skill. Despite the fact that the dry goods store stocked sewing material and even some apparel brought by wagon from the East, it was clear that most clothing and household linens were going to need to be fashioned by hand.

"I'm going to the Schroeders' as soon as the breakfast dishes are finished," she affirmed, knowing there were things she must learn that she had never dreamed of needing to do before. Most of the time, she welcomed the opportunity to spend time with Hannah and some of the other women, but her heart wasn't in it today. Not when a mile away, the streets teemed with adventure.

"Then you should stay there, where you belong, and not traipse about the streets, where Lord knows what might happen." Martha spoke as if the matter were settled.

"Roundup only comes once a year, my dear," Kate's father offered, seeing her disappointment. She knew he was as distracted by all the goings-on as she was, but he at least had the excuse of gathering information for the paper to explain his attendance at the events. "I'm sure that Mrs. Schroeder won't mind Kate's absence for a few days. I'll walk Kate over there myself just to make sure she arrives safely."

When Kate and her father arrived at Hannah's, they found her packing lunches. She explained that she had volunteered to watch one of the food tables and more than understood Kate's eagerness to observe the activities. When Kate promised to help her later that day, Hannah had shooed her off with John in tow, saying, "You two go on then. I'm 'most done here, and I've seen plenty of roundups. I don't mind missing a few hours of this one."

So by late morning, Kate was eagerly searching the crowds for a sign of Jessie Forbes. She was beginning to despair as she wended her way through throngs of men, down one dusty aisle after another, passing corral after corral filled with animals that all looked alike. The cowboys looked all of a kind, too. Broad-brimmed hats, vests over faded cotton shirts, dusty denim pants, and the ever-present leather chaps. Most had smudges of trail dirt on their faces, too, rendering them nearly interchangeable. Until Kate saw her.

Then she wondered how she had ever mistaken her for one of the cowboys just a few weeks before. Jessie, her face in profile to Kate, stood talking with a burly fellow twice her size. Even with the brim of her hat tipped down, throwing shadows over her eyes, her subtle grace was apparent. She was lean and taut, much like some of the younger men, but the gentle arch of her neck and the elegant curve of her jaw were inherently beautiful in a way that even the handsomest youth was not.

Jessie loosely clasped her gun belt in a familiar pose, and Kate studied those intriguing hands, fixing on the long, slender fingers. She remembered the careful way Jessie had held her hand the previous afternoon in the hotel, and her heart tripped a beat, her stomach making a sudden turn at the same time. Kate caught her breath, feeling suddenly, unaccountably, warm.

At that moment, Jessie looked her way. She smiled, and Kate smiled back, wondering at the rush of happiness that winged to her on that glorious smile. Jessie said something to the man she was with and hurried to Kate's side.

"Why, Kate! I didn't expect to see you here again today." She surveyed the nearby crowd. "Are you alone?"

"John Emory walked me down," Kate replied. "He's off with one of the wranglers just now."

Jessie grinned. "That boy has a real itch to be a cowboy. His father has something different in mind for him, I'll wager."

"Didn't yours?" Kate asked as they began to walk back toward the main arena where the auctioning was about to begin.

Her own parents had allowed her far more leniency than many of her girlfriends had enjoyed, letting her pursue her interest in photography, history, literature, and other subjects considered inappropriate for young women. But Kate couldn't imagine that Jessie's parents had approved of her working on the ranch. Even in this demanding place, where women were forced by circumstance to labor in ways their eastern cousins would find unthinkable, Kate had quickly recognized that women still did not, as a rule, determine their own destiny. She suspected that Jessie's father had harbored the same expectations as hers—that she find a suitable man to whom he could comfortably pass the responsibility of caring for and protecting her. "He must have wanted a secure life for you, not the hard and...and dangerous one of a rancher."

For a moment, Jessie looked puzzled. "Not that he ever said. Out here, settlers' children always work the land in some way or another. The littlest ones carry water and feed the stock, and the older ones rope and ride or plow, whatever needs to be done."

"The girls, too?" Kate asked carefully, thinking of the newspaper accounts she had read of the suffragettes in New York state, who were speaking out for a woman's right to vote and even own property. It wasn't a popular concept. Her mother had declared that these gatherings were unseemly and that no woman with any sense would want to take on the problems that went along with having that kind of say in things. Some things were best left to men.

"Well," Jessie continued, "if there's work to be done, everybody does it. Boys cook, and men help with the wash if need be, and come harvest time, every able body in the house—man, woman, or child—is in the field."

"And shooting game and herding horses?" Kate persisted.

Jessie grinned again. "I've seen some women who were damn fine shots with a rifle. As to the riding, that's almost required if you're going to get anywhere farther than town." She was suddenly serious. "My father taught me to be a rancher because I wanted to be. I don't remember much about my mother. She died of influenza when I was three. From the time I was small, I wanted to be like my father. Jed says I was riding before I could walk, and by the time I was seven, I had my first rifle. I liked school well enough, but I'd rather have been tending the herd out on the range. My father made me stay in school until I was fifteen, which is longer than any of the girls usually go. I'm glad now that he did."

Kate caught the wistful tone in Jessie's voice and sensed how much she missed her father. Kate ached for her loss, but she was struck, too, by Jessie's simple certainty. Jessie lived the life she loved. What an amazing thing. Kate walked along next to her in silence, wondering why, until now, she had never thought to question her own life and the path that had been preordained for her.

They stopped by the fence surrounding the main show ring, and Jessie leaned her back against the rail, studying her companion. Kate's dark eyes were distant, a touch of sadness clouding her usually animated features. "What's bothering you, Kate?"

She blushed. "Nothing. I was just thinking how much I envy you."

Jessie laughed, that deep melodious sound Kate found so lovely. "I doubt that you'd envy me after a night sleeping out in the cold, up some canyon with nothing for company but wolves and mountain goats."

Kate laughed, too. "You'll have to take me some time so I can find out for myself." She hesitated, then went on boldly, "Would you? Take me up there sometime?"

"Kate," Jessie said softly. "It's wild country no more than a few dozen miles from here. Beautiful, but heartless. It's hard even for those of us who have done it all our lives." She hated the look of disappointment that flickered across Kate's face. "But I'd be happy to show you around my ranch. Not much to see but the bunkhouse and the cook cabin and a bunch of pens, but if you'd like—"

"Oh, I'd love that," Kate affirmed. "Very much."

"Well, then, it's settled." Jessie pulled a watch from her pocket and frowned. "I'd better get along. I've got business waiting on me."

"I promised I'd help Mrs. Schroeder, too," Kate admitted reluctantly. "Good luck with the auction. I'll be thinking of you."

Jessie smiled, pleased. "Thank you, Kate."

"Goodbye, Jessie," Kate said softly. As she watched her walk away, she thought that the rest of the day could hold nothing as pleasant as these last few moments.

Kate had no chance to speak with Jessie again that morning, although she looked for her constantly. Once, she spied her at the corral deep in conversation with another rancher; the next time, Jessie was leading a horse around the pen while several men looked the animal over. Kate waved to her on several occasions when she could catch her eye, and Jessie smiled back and tipped her hat.

Most of the time, Kate was too busy at the refreshment tables or with her photography to keep track of anyone. There was no resident photographer in the territory, and people were constantly stopping to ask her questions. Many were skeptical that she could actually master such a complicated process, but that didn't stop them from asking if she could take their pictures. Kate found herself promising to take family shots for a number of neighbors after roundup ended. She had been working steadily much of the afternoon and finally stopped when the direct heat of the sun began to make her increasingly uncomfortable. She folded the camera's legs and dragged it over to one of the nearby food stands.

"You're going to take a stroke standing out there with that black cloth over your head," Hannah warned as Kate joined her. She handed her a lemonade drink, and Kate took it gratefully.

"You might be right," she gasped, chasing the dust from her throat with the tart beverage. "I've never had a chance to take photographs like this before. I don't want to miss a thing."

Hannah nodded. "I remember feeling that way, too, when we first arrived. When I wasn't scared to death, anyhow."

"What was it like?" Kate asked.

Hannah smiled wistfully. "Thaddeus thought he would be a homesteader, but one season on that damn prairie cured him of that. The winds in the summer blow hot enough to parch every blessed thing, and then in the winter, you freeze." She shook her head and moved the basket of food into a shadier spot on the table. "That land out there will kill you quick if you don't have a special love for it. And if it don't love you."

Kate immediately thought of Jessie, remembering the way she talked about her ranch. "Some people belong to it, I imagine."

Hannah looked at her oddly. "Don't you be listening to the stories those darn cowboys tell. It ain't so pretty when you're hip deep in snow and starving. It's bad enough that John Emory's got stars in his eyes about wanting to be a wrangler. Don't you go getting ideas!"

"Oh, don't worry," Kate said with a laugh. "I have no intention of becoming a cowboy."

As to listening to the cowboy stories, she thought she could listen forever if it were Jessie telling the tale.

CHAPTER SEVEN

After the third day of the roundup, Martha gave up trying to dissuade Kate from spending time at the auction stands and contented herself with her daughter's promise to keep out of the sun as much as possible.

"You'll ruin your skin," she warned.

Kate kissed her mother's cheek fondly and reached for the bonnet hanging on the coat tree by the door. "I'll wear it, don't fret!" she called as she hurried down the walk to the street.

She was eager to get there early because she wanted to find Jessie before the business of the day became too hectic. An idea had come over her the night before and she couldn't wait another minute to talk to Jessie about it. She headed straight for the area where she knew the Rising Star's livestock were corralled, searching for the rancher's distinctive form. When Kate saw her astride a great beast of a horse, she stopped to watch, standing back under the shade of a tree.

Jessie's face was all but indistinguishable under the low brim of her hat and the bandanna that covered her neck and mouth. She rode the horse hard from one end of the corral to the other, pulling back on the reins quickly several times to change direction and then leading his head in a tight circle so that his body nearly twisted on itself. He was powerfully built and gleamed black in the bright sunlight, a glorious mass of muscle and might.

It was the sight of Jessie, though, commanding him with the subtlest turn of her hands and the swift kick of her heels against his huge sides that captivated Kate. She stared at the way Jessie's thighs lifted slightly from the sweat-stained saddle as she leaned forward over his arching neck, urging him to run with the sheer force of her own will. Her breath quickened, and she was suddenly flushed, even though the air was still cool. She had never felt anything like this twisting, falling sensation in her belly before, and she would have been frightened if it hadn't been so terribly pleasant at the same time.

Her heart hammered, and she bit her lip to still its trembling. She leaned against the tree, welcoming its sturdy pressure against her back and struggled to steady her shaking legs. Maybe Hannah had been right in warning her against getting too much sun. Maybe she *was* suffering from heatstroke.

Jessie swung one leg down from the saddle and dropped easily to the ground, walking to the fence with the reins in one hand. The horse followed, snorting noisily from his run.

"He's a dandy, Jed," she announced to her foreman, who leaned against the rail of the corral. "He'd be a great line horse. He's got good legs and he never tires. I'm for buying him."

Jed nodded, chewing thoughtfully on a plug of tobacco. "If we could get us a mare or two like him, we'd have a solid start of a working brood line."

Jessie slapped her hat against her legs, causing great clouds of dust to rise from her chaps, then wiped her sleeve across her face, her mind working. "The railroads won't come this far north for a lot of years, and we'd have plenty of market for working horses with the stagecoaches running through here. I say we do it."

"Yep. Me, too."

"I'll go talk to Josiah Bradley about his mares this—" She stopped abruptly, staring past his shoulder, then tossed the reins over the fence rail and in the same motion braced both hands on the top rung. She vaulted up and over in an instant, bolting across the adjoining pasture, leaving Jed to stare after her in astonishment.

"Kate!" Jessie cried anxiously, skidding to a stop by her side. The young woman appeared pale and shaken. "Are you all right?"

Kate gave a tremulous smile. "Yes." She sounded a bit uncertain. "I think so. Perhaps a little too much sun."

Jessie glanced at the clear sky and felt the skitter of a breeze across her cheek. "It's not that warm, Kate," she said with concern, her fingers brushing Kate's hand. "You're shaking."

Kate met blue eyes dark with worry and took a deep breath, smiling for real. "I'm fine. Truly." She felt foolish now, appearing fragile when it wasn't that at all. She tried not to think about the fact that Jessie's light touch on her hand had started the falling sensations all over again. She pointed toward the corral, wanting to change the subject. "What was that you were doing in there?"

Jessie followed her gaze to where Jed was pulling the saddle off the stallion she had just ridden. "Working him out under saddle. I'm planning on buying him and a few others with similar bloodlines. I wanted to see how he'd handle."

Kate was afraid that anything she said would sound inane, but she didn't think she had ever seen anything as beautiful as Jessie Forbes on that horse. "I want to take your picture," she blurted.

"What? Me?" Jessie stared at Kate, astonished. Then she laughed. "Oh, Kate! Why on earth would you want to do that? With all this beautiful country around here, you want to take a picture of a dusty trail hand?"

"You're beautiful, too," Kate said quite seriously. When Jessie blushed, she hurried on. "You are—I mean—the way you looked on that horse, like the two of you were born connected. It's...it's..." She stopped in frustration. *Why is it so hard to put words to the way I feel about you?*

"Kate," Jessie said quietly. "If it would please you to take my picture, then I won't say no."

Kate's brilliant smile was Jessie's reward. "This afternoon?"

"Whenever you want." Jessie laughed again. "Should I change my clothes? I'll be riding all morning, and by then I'll be a sight."

Remembering how Jessie had looked in a sweat-dampened shirt, Kate shook her head. "No," she said softly, shyly now. "I want you just like that."

"Millie, could you let me have two of your sandwiches?" Kate asked. "I'll spell you here tomorrow morning in return."

Millie was a new bride, the young wife of the town marshal. She was rumored to make the best brisket in town, and her stand was a popular one with the cowboys. She had been one of the first women in New Hope to befriend Kate, and being of a similar age, they made easy companions.

"Of course." Millie regarded Kate with a knowing smile. "Two sandwiches, is it? You aren't trying to bribe your way into some man's heart, are you?"

Kate colored self-consciously. "No, I'm taking one for Jessie Forbes."

"Well," Millie announced, packing a basket, "if she's anything like my Tom after a day on a horse, you'd best take three."

"Thank you, Millie," Kate said, gathering the basket of food.

"Of course, silly. Oh! Don't forget the dance tomorrow night. Everyone will be there."

Kate smiled, her eyes fixed on the auction yard, her mind on Jessie. "I won't forget."

It was the biggest auction day of the week, and the yard was packed. Kate walked to the edge of the crowd surrounding the auction platform. She watched as several prize steers, or so the auctioneer claimed, were auctioned off at apparently high prices. Kate found it hard to follow the bidding because men seemed to signal without saying anything.

"Now, gentlemen," the auctioneer called. "The last sale of the afternoon, and the one you've been waiting for, I imagine. I'm offering the best brood mare this side of the Mississippi. She's gonna throw the finest foals this territory has ever seen. Do I hear an opening bid?"

A murmur passed through the crowd, and Kate saw Jessie, across the yard, touch her hat brim nonchalantly. She had one heel up on the railing and was leaning an arm over the top post, looking relaxed and casual. The bidding became rapid, and Kate lost track of the amount, but every now and then she saw Jessie touch her hat. Finally the bidding slowed, and the crowd quieted.

"Do I hear another bid, gentlemen?" the auctioneer called. "Any other bids? Going once, going twice, SOLD!" He looked Jessie's way and shouted, "To the Rising Star ranch!"

Jessie broke into a smile and turned to the cowboy beside her, who pumped her hand vigorously before walking off toward the holding pens. As the crowd started to disperse, Kate picked her way carefully across the rutted ground.

Jessie watched her approach, too happy to contain a wide grin. "Hello, Kate."

Kate was always surprised at the deep, mellow quality of Jessie's voice. She tilted her head back to look up into her face and said a little breathlessly, "Is that the horse you wanted?"

"Yep, she is. I've been waiting almost two years to find the right animal, and this is the one."

"I'm glad for you," Kate said, meaning it. She lifted her napkin draped wicker basket. "I brought some sandwiches. If you're going to pose for me, I thought I should feed you first."

Jessie looked surprised and then pleased. "I could do with something to eat. I've been so worked up over the bidding today I think I forgot all about my stomach." She frowned. "Where's your camera and all?"

"I left it back at the tables. We can get it after we eat."

"I'm about ready for that right now."

Impulsively, Kate threaded her arm through Jessie's. "Good. Then let's find a nice quiet place to celebrate your new purchase."

For an instant, Jessie went utterly still. The nearness of Kate's body was completely strange to her. She never would have thought that the soft touch of a woman's hand could make her feel so tall.

"I think that's a fine idea, Kate," she said softly.

A short walk from town, they found a secluded spot under a cluster of elms, and Jessie helped Kate spread out a cloth on the ground. At their backs, the foothills rose precipitously toward the towering mountain range that blotted out great patches of the deep blue sky. Here and there dollops of white frothy clouds hid the peaks or floated free to decorate the heavens. There were no sounds save for the faint buzzing of insects and the faraway lowing of cattle in the auction pens.

"I'm glad that you suggested we bring the camera with us," Kate said, unfolding the legs of the support. "Now that we're here, I don't want to go back for anything. It's a perfect spot, and I can't wait to get started."

Jessie watched the process, hands in her back pockets, a curious look on her face. "I still think my horses would make a prettier picture."

Kate merely smiled and gestured to a spot where she could use the mountain as a backdrop. "Right over there, please." She positioned the camera, framing Jessie in the foreground. "No, leave your hat on. Just tip it back a bit." She looked up, meeting Jessie's gaze. "I like you in that hat."

The hint of teasing, and something else—something warm—in Kate's voice, caused Jessie to blush. "What should I do with my hands?" she asked to cover her embarrassment.

Kate lifted the cloth over her head and, in a muffled voice called, "Just stand like you were talking to Jed. Pretend I'm not here."

"That would be some kind of trick, for sure," Jessie muttered.

Kate laughed. "And don't talk."

Through the lens, she focused on Jessie. Isolated under the black covering, Kate was alone with her in a way that was so strangely intimate it made her pulse flutter. She was struck anew by Jessie's confident carriage and supple strength. The rancher was unlike anyone, man or woman, Kate had ever known. She was so beautiful it made Kate's throat ache.

With a trembling hand, she opened the shutter and began to count softly to herself. For a few seconds after she finished the exposure, she continued to gaze at her, absorbing every detail of her face and body. Finally she called, "We're done." Her voice sounded strange to her own ears, and she was aware of an unsettling warmth in her depths.

"Can't say as I mind," Jessie remarked, but her tone was light. She stretched out on the ground next to the makeshift tablecloth, enjoying the breeze that played over her face, and was inexplicably content. "Seems like an age since I've stopped more than a minute in one spot."

Kate sat down beside her, bringing the basket of food and placing it between them. She studied Jessie's face, catching the weary undertones in her voice. Jessie had tossed her hat behind her and lay on her back, one arm behind her head, her long legs sprawled out in front of her. Her eyes were closed, her hair a thick golden mane that framed her tanned face, just touching her collar. A patch of pale skin on her upper chest that the sun hadn't touched was exposed where the shirt fell open. She looked terribly vulnerable, and Kate suddenly realized that for all Jessie's ability and strength, she was still but a woman barely older than herself. *And a very tired one.*

"Are you all right, Jessie?" she asked, her voice husky with concern.

Jessie turned her head, her lids fluttering open, and found herself looking up into Kate's deep, dark eyes. For a moment she did not answer. Kate's skin was the most beautiful color that she had ever seen, rich as fresh cream. Her black hair and brows emphasized her loveliness, and Jessie was reminded of a picture of angels she had seen in one of her father's books. Just now, however, Kate's eyes were cloudy, and a little frown line was etched just above her nose. Jessie smiled then, a brilliant smile that chased the shadows from Kate's eyes.

"I'm fine, Kate. This has been a hard week for my ranch. I've sold or traded most of my stock, and there were a few deals I wasn't sure I could make. But I think it's over now."

"You'll be leaving soon, won't you?" Kate's expression darkened again. The thought of how dull and empty her days would be without a few moments with Jessie to look forward to made her sad—an aching sadness she'd never once felt even upon leaving Boston and her whole life behind.

Jessie leaned up on one elbow, nodding. "We'll head back to the ranch the day after tomorrow. The men have let off some steam, and we all have a lot of work to do when we get back."

"Of course." Kate looked away, her hands tightening in her lap. "I see."

Now Jessie was troubled. Seeing Kate upset bothered her more than she could say. "Kate, what's wrong?"

Kate turned to Jessie, her cheeks flushed. "Oh Jessie, don't pay any attention to me. It's just that all this will be over then." Her eyes were suddenly, inexplicably, swimming with tears. "And—and you'll be gone, too," she finished softly.

"Kate, I–I…" Jessie hesitantly touched the back of her hand to the single drop that had escaped Kate's long lashes, trailing unheeded down her cheek. A tightness in her chest grew so heavy she thought she would stop breathing. "Kate," she whispered.

"Shh." Kate placed her fingers gently on Jessie's. "Never mind. It's not your fault."

The air grew thick, and a fine tremor began in Jessie's fingers. Her head buzzed like it did when she'd been too long in the saddle in the August heat.

Time stopped for Kate, every sound stilled, as she gazed at Jessie, frozen. She could see so clearly the quick rise and fall of her chest beneath the cotton shirt. She wanted desperately to run her fingers over the bruise that still lingered on Jessie's cheek, but she didn't dare move. If Jessie took her hand from Kate's skin, Kate feared she would die. She knew her face was high with color, but all she could think about was Jessie's eyes. *How can anyone's eyes be so blue?*

Jessie's eyes locked with Kate's. Mesmerized, she felt as if she were falling with nothing to hold on to. Her legs trembled so much she could not have stood if a herd of horses was drawing down on her. Something inside her stirred, hungry and scared all at once. Her blood ran hot and fierce with a want for which she had no name. She pulled away, warring with an army of sensations she had never known.

Kate's hand fell back into her lap.

"The sandwiches..." Jessie mumbled, reaching blindly toward the basket.

"Yes," Kate answered, her voice unsteady. "We should..."

They avoided looking at one another as they ate, their usual easy conversation now halting and self-conscious. Once, when Kate brushed Jessie's hand by accident, they both jumped. With lunch finally over, they walked back into town in silence, and Jessie deposited Kate's camera near Millie's table.

"You will come to the dance, won't you?" Kate asked finally as they prepared to part. They stood very close, but did not touch. "Before you go?"

Jessie nodded. "I'll be there."

"Promise?" Kate hid her anxiety with a smile. *Oh, how I don't want you to go.*

"I promise," Jessie said with an answering smile of her own.

Kate did touch her then, a light brush of her fingers along Jessie's arm. "Good."

Jessie watched Kate turn away, saw Millie take Kate's arm and draw her into conversation with a young man from town, and wondered why it seemed like something was tearing loose inside her. She walked away in the gathering dusk, feeling more alone than she could ever remember.

CHAPTER EIGHT

M artha! We'll be late if we don't leave soon!"
Martin and Kate were impatiently pacing the length of
the sitting room, dressed and ready to go. Martin didn't want to miss
a moment of the night's festivities. Kate hadn't been able to think of
anything all day except that this was Jessie's last night in town and it
would be so dreary after she and the other cowboys left.

"Well, Kate, since almost everyone in town will be at the dance
tonight, it will be like your coming-out ball all over again." He smiled
at his daughter approvingly. "You look lovely."

She wore a midnight-blue evening dress that she had carefully
packed and carried all the way from Boston. Even though dark blue
was not the usual choice for young unmarried women, Kate loved the
color, and her mother had relented and allowed her to wear it. It was
cut away at the neck to reveal a hint of décolletage, with the skirt styled
closer in the front after the latest fashions in the East to flatter the figure.
Kate had worn it once before but not with the anticipation she did now.
Tonight, in her rustling gown and with her arms quite naked beneath
long white kid gloves, she felt like a woman and not like a young girl
on display.

"I hardly think it will be anything as grand as the party you and
Mother arranged for my seventeenth birthday," Kate said graciously,
"but I *am* looking forward to seeing my new friends this evening." *And
Jessie. Jessie most of all.*

"I'm certain that after this evening, we'll be seeing more than a
few young men appearing at our door," Martin enthused, beaming with

fatherly pride.

Kate smiled at him, dismissing the question of suitors with an easy shrug. "We shall never know if we don't get there. I'll go see what's keeping Mother."

She left her father peering at his watch and made her way upstairs to her mother's room. Martha was seated before her dressing table, dressed to go.

"Mother! Is something wrong? Are you ill?" Kate asked, taken aback by the look of distress on her mother's face.

"No, I'm not ill. Merely frightened, I think." Martha smiled wanly. "You and your father have settled in so well, it's as if you've always lived here. But I still feel like a stranger."

"A stranger! The house is always filled with visitors, and the neighbors have been so welcoming," Kate protested.

"Oh, I know. Everyone *is* kind and helpful, but I still feel out of place. Tonight, with the whole town there, I'm not sure I can manage."

"You expect too much of yourself, Mother." Kate crossed the room and put her hands on her mother's shoulders sympathetically. "There's no hurry. You'll discover in time that these people are really no different than those we knew in Boston. You have to look past their clothes and their different ways and see them for the honest, good people that they are." She met her mother's gaze in the mirror. "I don't expect you'll like all of them, but I think you'll find most of them can be friends. Some of them are quite extraordinary."

"Indeed they are." Martha found a small smile.

Kate's dark eyes sparkled at her. "Come on now, before Father explodes!"

She looks so grown up, Martha thought, *and it's not just the dress or her new hairstyle.* She noted absently that Kate had forgone the customary tight curls for a simpler, looser style pulled back toward the crown, leaving her neck quite bare save for a few ringlets. It was perhaps a bit too daring, but Martha was too taken with the confidence that radiated from Kate to mention it. *I've never seen her so happy. Why, she's positively glowing. She'll be turning all the young men's heads tonight. And I mustn't keep her from that.*

Martha stood and took Kate's arm. "It will be a wonderful night, I'm sure. Let's go rescue your father from his impatience."

She followed her daughter downstairs, far from certain about the evening to come but determined to make the best of her situation. It was clear that her husband and her daughter had already made New Hope their home.

Jessie packed her valise and stood it at the foot of the bed. She planned to leave in the morning and had already settled her accounts at the bank. She'd only stayed tonight because of the town gathering and dance. It was a town tradition to celebrate the end of roundup, and despite the fact that she didn't know most of the townspeople any more than to say hello, she had been raised to respect tradition. And she had promised Kate that she would be there.

Just thinking of Kate made her smile. The time they'd spent together had seemed so much more exciting than anything she'd ever done before. As much as she loved running the ranch, as much as this land was in her blood, she'd never come across anything that made her feel so alive as being with Kate. No one had ever made her feel at once so comfortable and so exhilarated. She knew there were other feelings Kate stirred in her, but not knowing how to explain them, she set them aside.

She didn't understand why being with Kate felt so natural and so good, and she supposed it didn't matter. Soon, she would be back at the ranch, and she would probably never see Kate again, except to nod hello in the street when they might happen to meet. Unaccountably saddened by that realization, she turned to the mirror above the dresser and surveyed her reflection, determined not to think about anything except the evening ahead.

She wore a black shirt with silver trim at the pockets and cuffs, tucked into close-fitting black pants. Her blond hair was tied loosely at the back of her neck with a black ribbon. The heavy beaten silver trim on her ornate holster matched the shimmering silver threads in her shirt. *I look like a tenderfoot,* she thought ruefully, but she was not displeased. Reaching for her black Stetson, she walked out and closed her door.

She heard the sounds of revelry from blocks away. The crowd spilled out of the meetinghouse into the street, and music and the muted roar of many voices poured out through the open double doors. She sidled her way through the crowd, nodding and exchanging hellos with wranglers she knew and townspeople she recognized. Once inside the large crowded room, she made her way slowly around the periphery. In the center of the space, people jostled and talked and surrounded those couples dancing to the lively music of several fiddlers.

Nearing the tables in the rear where women offered food and drink, she suddenly realized that she was very hungry. A robust arm reached out for her, and she turned, meeting twinkling blue eyes and a broad smile.

"Jessie Forbes! You look mighty fine tonight," Hannah Schroeder bellowed above the roar. "I heard that you did well at the auction this year. I'm pleased to hear it!"

Jessie broke into a smile and shouted back, "Thank you, and your husband, too. I would say I'm pleased enough with how the Rising Star did!"

Hannah nodded again and piled food on a plate. As she handed it to Jessie, she seemed to remember something and shouted again, "Jessie, I forgot to introduce you two. This here is Mrs. Martin Beecher. She and her family are new in town. Martha, this is Jessie Forbes, one of the ranchers from north of here."

Jessie looked quickly at Martha, who was staring at her intently, and doffed her hat. She could see the resemblance to Kate in that dark hair and penetrating gaze. "Ma'am," she said politely. "I'm pleased to know you. I hope you're settling in well."

Martha struggled to absorb the idea of a woman striding about in public dressed like a man and carrying a weapon. *Different, Kate said? Indecent is more like it. Lord, what are people thinking of out here!*

She answered stiffly, "How do you do, Miss Forbes." She turned away gratefully when a new arrival extended a plate for her to fill. All she could think was how relieved she would be when all this roundup business was over and these cowboys left town.

Unabashed, Jessie stared after her for a second. She then thanked Hannah and moved off to a quiet corner of the room to eat.

Kate had been watching the door all evening, waiting for Jessie to arrive, and when she first saw her, she caught her breath sharply in surprise. She had not known what to expect, but certainly not this. Jessie appeared neither as a dusty trail hand nor as another frontier woman in her best Sunday dress. She was just herself—striking in shimmering black and silver, confident and sure. She stood slightly apart from the crowd and, in Kate's eyes, was the most interesting person in the room. Kate stepped quietly away from the group of young women she was with and made her way through the crowd toward her.

Jessie leaned back against a broad wooden pole, a little away from the edge of the dance floor, listening to the fiddlers alternate between lively dance tunes and slow, mournful ballads. Relaxing didn't come easy to her, not in a crowded room wearing her best clothes, but the cool evening breeze drifting in from an open window carried the scent of the land, and that helped settle her. She looked over the crowd, searching for Kate. She hadn't thought about much else all day except that she would see Kate that night. She was alternately jubilant and worried about the prospect. Memories of their strange lunch the day before kept plaguing her. It seemed as if they'd gone from being easy with one another to awkward in the blink of an eye, and she couldn't recall a thing she might have said to upset Kate. And she'd thought hard on it. But she was clear on one fact—Kate had been troubled when they parted, and that troubled *her* more than anything ever had.

At that moment, Jessie spied her and forgot completely what she had been fretting about. Gliding toward her in a gown the likes of which she'd never seen, Kate was a vision, easily the loveliest woman in the room. The smile Kate sent Jessie's way set her heart to pounding as if she'd just run a race.

"I thought you might not come!" Kate declared breathlessly.

"And what else would I do during the biggest gathering of the year?" Jessie's teasing grin grew a little shy. "Besides, I told you that I would be here."

"Yes, you did," Kate said softly, her eyes holding Jessie's. She knew absolutely that this woman would always keep her word. "I was silly to worry."

Jessie was surprised by the wistful note in her voice. "Is something wrong?"

"No," Kate answered with a quick shake of her head. She was determined to enjoy their time together; she'd been thinking of nothing else for days. "Everything is fine."

"Good," Jessie said, smiling. "I'm so glad to see you."

"You look beautiful tonight. I like you in black." As she spoke, Kate realized she really meant it. Even though Jessie had a way of capturing her attention with little more than a smile, Kate found her particularly attractive in her unconventional finery. She didn't ordinarily give serious notice to fashion, but Jessie looked so different than any of the other women. So certain and strong. *And, yes, beautiful.*

Blushing under her tan, Jessie looked away. She wasn't used to the kind of admiring glance Kate was giving her. It seemed as if she could feel Kate's eyes moving over her body, and it was doing funny things to her breathing.

When she spoke, her voice was thick and low. "I'd say *beautiful* was more what you are tonight, Kate." Her pulse raced as her gaze traveled from Kate's eyes, dark and deep with feeling, to her full lips, curved now into a faint smile. Dimly, she was aware of blood pounding in her ears as she watched the hypnotic rise and fall of Kate's breasts against the brilliant blue of the dress. "You...shine."

Kate couldn't look away from her. The sound of Jessie's voice was all that she could hear, the blue of Jessie's eyes all that she could see. She took a step closer. Her head was level with Jessie's shoulder; she watched the pulse beat quickly in Jessie's neck, dizzy with the urge to rest her fingertips there.

Jessie could barely breathe. Her right hand was curled so tightly around her silver studded belt, her fingers ached. She drew breath in sharply as she felt Kate's fingers come to rest feather light upon her own, but she didn't move. Kate's eyes were sparkling black diamonds, and her face was misted with a fine perspiration. Jessie looked down, stunned to see Kate's hand curve around hers. The gentle touch made her ache inside, as if she were terribly empty and desperate to be filled. She didn't know for what she longed, but she knew she wanted that touch to never end.

"Kate," she whispered.

"Jessie..." Kate lifted her other hand slowly, intent on caressing the pulse fluttering hypnotically in Jessie's throat. Her hand, inches from Jessie's skin, fingers trembling faintly, was stilled by an intruding voice quite near.

"Why, Miss Beecher..."

Jessie jerked her head around as the man beside them continued, "You look too pretty tonight to be standing off here all alone. I think you should be dancing. May I have that pleasure?" Ken Turner, the town's only lawyer and himself a relative newcomer, flashed a confident smile at Kate and waited expectantly.

"I'm not alone!" Kate retorted hotly, not bothering to hide her anger at his rude intrusion. "I'm talking with—"

"He's right, Kate." Jessie quickly pulled her hand from beneath Kate's and took a step back. "This is a party, and you *should* be dancing.

You go ahead."

"But I—"

"Go on," Jessie repeated softly.

Kate was unable to decipher the remote expression in Jessie's eyes, and she didn't know how to politely refuse Ken Turner's request. Although leaving Jessie to dance with him was the last thing she wanted to do, she understood that it was expected of her. Nodding a silent assent to the man who stood regarding her with confident anticipation, she took his arm, letting him lead her to the dance floor. As she followed, she struggled with her anger and confusion. She did not want to dance with him, and despite the dictates of propriety, it upset her that Jessie insisted that she should. Feigning civility as he placed his arm lightly around her waist, Kate stole a glance around his shoulder to where Jessie had been standing. The pain was swift and sharp when she saw that she was gone.

Jessie shouldered through the swinging doors of the saloon and surveyed the empty room. Even Frank the bartender was at the dance. She sidled behind the bar and poured a brandy, leaving a coin on the polished top. Tucking the bottle under her arm, she walked to the nearest table, pulled out a chair, and sat down. She alternately sipped her drink and stared into the amber liquid, refilling the glass automatically when it was empty. She wasn't sure how long she'd been there when she heard footsteps on the stairs behind her.

"Well, Montana," Mae softly called as she made her way behind the bar. She pulled a bottle down from the shelf. "You're home early from the dance."

"I didn't much feel like it tonight, Mae."

"Oh? And everyone's there, too."

"Yep," Jessie said with a sigh. "Big crowd."

Mae frowned at Jessie's impassive expression, wondering at the hollow tone in her voice. She poured herself a whiskey and came around the bar to sit down on Jessie's right. Casually, she put her hand on Jessie's arm. "Something happen tonight, Jess?"

"What?" Jessie asked, as if from far away. She couldn't find the words to describe how she felt, even to herself. Empty, in a funny sort of way. Not like being hungry—more like being lost and cold. "Oh…

no. Just tired, I guess."

"I don't know," Mae teased lightly. "Maybe you've had too much of this easy town living. Might be you're just homesick for a rocky bed and bad food." She sipped the whiskey and watched her friend's face, knowing Jessie was too honest to hide the truth for long.

Jessie regarded Mae fondly. "Maybe that's it. Too much comfort can be bad for you." She stretched her legs out under the table and shrugged her tense shoulders. "Maybe I *do* just need to get back to the ranch where I belong."

Mae rose to stand behind Jessie's chair, placing both hands lightly on her tight shoulders. Gently kneading the stiff muscles, she leaned close to murmur, "Tell you what *I* think you need. A good old-fashioned bath."

Eyes closed, Jessie sighed softly and titled her head back. Mae's hands felt good, and she *was* weary. "You'll have me asleep here in a minute, Mae."

"You just wait on that, cowboy," Mae instructed lightly, continuing her massage. "One of the girls was just drawing me a hot tub upstairs. The way these muscles are strung, you feel like you could use it more than me. Finish your drink now. "

"Don't know as I want to move," Jessie said drowsily. The liquor and gentle ministrations combined to lull her into a welcome torpor.

Mae stared down at Jessie's finely chiseled features and stroked her fingers lightly over the silky smooth skin of her neck. Minutes passed and Jessie remained motionless, her slender hands resting quietly on her thighs, her head resting gently against Mae's body.

Finally moving her hand, Mae whispered with effort, "Come on, Montana. I'll give you a hand with that bath."

Jessie shuddered and roused herself. She followed Mae slowly up the stairs, but her mind was still on the dance and the way that Kate had looked in Ken Turner's arms. She had no idea why it bothered her so much that she wouldn't get to say goodbye.

"Shed those duds," Mae instructed as she tested the temperature of the water, then added a little more from a still-steaming kettle sitting on the fireplace hearth in the far corner of the room. "And climb in here."

Paying no mind to Mae's casual glance, Jessie stripped wearily and laid her clothes over the chair next to the bed. With a groan, she lowered herself into the tin tub. "That does feel good."

Mae stood behind her, working up a lather with a bar of soap. "Dunk your head."

Jessie did, then shook the water from her eyes and rested her neck on the rim, stretching her arms out along the sides of the tin tub. The water came to just above her breasts. She closed her eyes once more as Mae washed her hair, murmuring softly in appreciation. Drifting with the heat and the soothing rhythm of Mae's fingers on her scalp, she skirted the edge of sleep.

Watching as Jessie's limbs loosened and her breathing became slow and deep, Mae gently rinsed the soap from thick sun-streaked hair, smoothing the stray strands off Jessie's face. She rested her palms very lightly on Jessie's shoulders, her fingers trailing over the edge of collarbone, just brushing the pale skin of her upper chest. Jessie shifted and sighed. Mae held her breath for a long moment, her hands trembling, then murmured, "Jessie."

Jessie heard the soft voice call to her from a long ways away. She smiled up into the face so close to hers, responding to the welcoming gaze with a swift rush of pleasure. She lifted her hand and caught the fingers that stroked her skin, turning the palm and pressing it to her lips. She was warm, warm and liquid deep within, and her limbs trembled with a sweet urgency that grew more insistent as she drew the hand she held onto her breast. She tilted her head, eager for a kiss from the lips so near her own. With the first gentle pressure on her mouth, she moaned quietly, the breath stealing from her body on the wings of desire.

"Wake up, Montana," Mae repeated, louder this time.

Jessie came awake with a start, sitting up so suddenly that water splashed over the rim onto the floor. "Lord," she muttered, looking wildly about. Mae stood beside her, a towel in her hand. "What happened?"

"You fell asleep," Mae said matter-of-factly.

"That's all?" Jessie asked, trying to piece together the fragments of the dream. All she could clearly recall were wisps of color—blue skies, white bits of clouds, and dark eyes boring into her. Eyes that were very different from Mae's deep green ones. Her body quivered strangely, and she thought her skin might catch fire from the inside. She drew a ragged breath, reached for the towel, and stepped from the tub on trembling legs. "You sure?"

"What else?" Mae inquired, heading for the door. She wasn't about to tell Jessie whose name she had murmured in her sleep. There wasn't any point to giving her ideas if she didn't already have them. The one way Jessie differed from the cowboys she rode with was that she was sweetly unschooled in matters of the flesh. Mae loved Jessie's innocence as much as it sometimes tried her. "Go on to bed now. You were just dreaming, Jess."

Jessie stared at the door as it closed behind her friend, the memory of a kiss still tingling on her lips.

CHAPTER NINE

"K ate, Kate darling!" Martha called. "You must go upstairs and get ready. Mr. Turner will be here for dinner any moment, and you don't want him finding you like that!" She frowned as Kate turned away from the window where she'd been sitting most of the afternoon, silent and withdrawn.

As her daughter disappeared obediently upstairs, Martha turned to Martin, who sat before the fireplace, engrossed in the paper. "I'm worried about Kate. She has been so quiet these last few weeks. She spends most of her time in that darkroom with her pictures, and she rarely visits any of her new friends. I do believe she's losing weight. She needs to get out more."

Martin chuckled. "Haven't you noticed all this mooning about started shortly after the dance last month? Just about the time young Ken Turner started calling? I should think you'd recognize the way a young girl acts when she's being courted." He smiled. "And I must say, I like that Turner. He's got a fine head on his shoulders and a promising future in this town. He'd make a very good husband for Kate."

Exasperated, Martha wasn't as convinced as her husband as to the cause of Kate's moodiness. She indeed knew how young girls in love acted. They might moon about, but only when it suited them. She saw none of the excitement in Kate's eyes that should have been there when Ken Turner came to call, and no eagerness for his visits. The lawyer gave every indication that his intent was serious where Kate was concerned. Kate, for her part, was polite, modest, and attentive, as was proper and expected under the circumstances. But when alone, she was melancholic.

"I'm not so sure, Martin. Kate isn't acting at all like herself." Martha hoped her daughter hadn't gotten some romantic notion about love being more important than practicality. Marriage was the first priority. Fondness would follow, as it had for her and Martin.

Martin sighed and went to his wife, putting his arms around her. "Don't worry, my dear. No reason in the world why she shouldn't take to Ken Turner. Given time, she'll see that, too."

❖

"I'm sorry," Kate said, blushing. "What did you say?"

Sitting with her parents and Ken Turner in the parlor after dinner, Kate found her mind wandering. She was restless and had a hard time paying attention to the usual topics of conversation that invariably included discussions of the weather, the newspaper business, and the increasing lawlessness along the Overland Trail. As the conversation went on around her, she wondered why she wasn't feeling what she should for Ken Turner. He had all the attributes of a proper suitor. He was pleasant and amusing, and her parents approved of him.

However, when he looked at her with fond regard, she felt like a bird in a trap. She wanted to flee, from his appraising glances and her parents' expectant expressions. Yet, with ever-deepening dread, she realized that she had nowhere to go. She tried to imagine being married to him, for surely that was why he continued to call, and she couldn't. She could not imagine waking up next to him in the morning or talking with him over breakfast, and she could not, no matter how hard she tried, imagine lying with him in the night. When he kissed her cheek before leaving in the evening, she had to force herself not to recoil from his touch.

"I'm sorry?" she repeated.

"Mr. Turner was asking about the help you've been giving Millie down at the school," Martha chided gently.

"Oh! Yes," Kate replied, trying to sound enthusiastic. In truth, helping Millie Roberts was the only thing preserving her sanity, or so it seemed to her. "There are so many more children now, and since she's expecting her own soon, Millie needs help. I've been teaching reading, and I love it."

"Admirable," Ken remarked heartily. "A very fine thing for you to do until a regular teacher can be found and you yourself are married."

Kate stared at him, at a loss as to how to respond. It was true that teaching was usually considered an occupation for unmarried women, since women rarely held any kind of employment after marriage. Millie, she knew, had only stayed on because the town hadn't been able to find a replacement. She had never understood why marriage meant a woman could not work outside the home, and as she considered her own future, it made even less sense. She could not see herself living her mother's life or even the lives of friends like Millie. *What is wrong with me?*

She looked at the handsome young man in her parents' parlor and thought about the evening they had met. The only thing she could recall about the entire event was a tall, blond woman in black and silver. *Jessie.* Kate hadn't even had the chance to say goodbye.

The morning after the dance, she had hurried to the hotel, asking for Jessie, only to be told the rancher was gone. She had rushed through town to the auction yards, desolate when she found that the pens were all empty. With a sinking feeling, she had surveyed the open gates and the deserted corrals. Right then, a sadness had settled upon her that would not lift. She ached, and she longed for something she could not name.

She had not seen Jessie in the month since, but the memory of her was as clear as one of her photos. She kept looking for her every time a cowboy rode into town or she heard the jingle of spurs on the sidewalk behind her. When she lay down to sleep, she remembered the glow in Jessie's eyes as they stood close together, their hands lightly touching. She would find that she was shivering, first hot, then cold, her heart racing. Her dreams were filled with strange half-visions of long, slender fingers, golden hair, and blue, blue eyes. She would awaken in the morning even more unsettled, with a curious trembling in her stomach. *What is happening?*

"Kate, Kate!" Martha looked at her daughter with concern. "Mr. Turner has asked to see some of your photos, dear."

Kate forced a bright smile. "Of course! How kind. I'll bring some out for you." She escaped gratefully to her room, counting the minutes until she could be alone again.

❖

Jessie paced uneasily back and forth on the broad porch that fronted her home. It was late, and the night was still under a black sky broken only by the faraway flicker of summer stars. For some reason, she couldn't read; her mind kept losing the thread. Her insides were churning, and even a bit of whiskey couldn't settle her. She had taken to riding hours on the open range every day, checking fences that didn't need mending and riding herd on horses that didn't need tending. She slept poorly and was short-tempered, flaring up at Jed over nothing at all. Even the sight of the sun setting over the land she loved failed to calm her. This land, her home, which had always been her comfort, seemed empty and barren.

The sound of her boots on the wood floors echoed aimlessly off the walls, and she was lonely. She sighed deeply and looked about her. She was tired, but she knew she wouldn't sleep. Instead, she walked to the barn and saddled her horse. She'd ride more, and maybe she'd no longer feel the ache.

Hours later, she dismounted in front of the saloon in New Hope. It was near to closing, and the bar was almost empty when she entered. She smiled wanly at Frank's surprised face as she leaned against the bar. "Evening, Frank. Got any of that brandy left?"

"Sure thing, Jessie. Kind of surprised to see you in here tonight."

"Me, too. I just started out from the ranch, and this is where I ended up."

He didn't comment. He'd been a bartender long enough to know that sometimes a cowboy just got tired of the silence out there in the night. He poured her a drink and filled her in on some of the local news.

Jessie listened and nodded, letting the warm glow of the brandy take the worry from her mind.

"Buy a lady a drink, Montana?"

Jessie smiled, her spirits lifting. She glanced sideways. "I sure will, if you'll sit and drink it with me, Mae."

Mae's sharp glance took in the circles under Jessie's eyes and the uneasy expression even the liquor couldn't smooth away. "You know there's nothing I'd like better, Jess. What brings you in here this time of week? Ranching getting too quiet for you?"

"Couldn't sleep," she admitted. "Didn't know what I wanted 'til I ended up here."

"Oh?" Mae's eyebrows arched as she said in a slightly mocking tone, "And what might that be?"

Jessie flushed, suddenly shy. "A friendly voice and a warm smile, I think."

Mae took Jessie's arm in hers and led her to a corner table. She lifted her glass to her lips and stared intently into Jessie's troubled eyes. "I'd say you've got something on your mind. Want to talk about it?"

"I don't know. I haven't been right lately, Mae. You know I love the ranch, and the work has always made me happy. These last few weeks I've felt sort of uneasy, like something was missing. Can't seem to get my head clear." Jessie looked down at the table, confused.

"Maybe you're just expecting too much from yourself. Work can't be everything to a person. I'd say you need a little relaxing now and then. Never could figure how a body could work as hard as you do."

Jessie laughed and tipped her brandy glass. Suddenly, she didn't feel quite so alone. She bought them both another drink, and they sat and talked and waited for the sun to come up.

Finally, Jessie arched her back and looked out toward the street. "Lord! I've kept you up the whole night!"

A small smile played across Mae's face. She swallowed the last of her drink and answered slowly, "Can't think of anyone else I'd rather spend the night with, Jess."

Jessie looked into her green eyes and felt herself grinning like a fool. "I'll remember that, Mae."

As she walked Jessie to the door and watched her stride off into the morning, Mae answered softly, "You be sure and do that, Montana."

CHAPTER TEN

Martin groaned softly and turned over, struggling to ignore the pounding in his head. At last, he gave in and opened one eye. It was then that he realized that the barrage was coming from his front porch. He reached for his watch on the nightstand and was astounded to see that it was not yet six in the morning.

"Who could that be?" Martha queried anxiously from beside him as she sat up, the coverlet clutched protectively to her chest.

"I'll go see," he muttered, searching on the floor for his slippers.

Kate's bedroom door opened, and she peeked out, bleary-eyed and confused. "What is it?"

Martin shook his head, trudging sleepily to the stairs. "Don't know, my dear."

Kate pulled her robe tightly closed over her nightgown and followed her father down the stairs. Through the curtains covering the window in the front door, she recognized Thaddeus Schroeder's large form. He was raising his fist to bang again on the frame, simultaneously rattling the doorknob. The entire door shook on its hinges.

"Wait a minute!" Martin bellowed as he fit the key to the lock.

"Martin!" Thaddeus shouted before the door was half open. "Get dressed. We've got to put out a special edition of the paper! There's news, man!"

"What's happened?" Martin asked, instantly awake and turning back toward the stairs. "Let me get into some clothes."

Thaddeus followed into the foyer, calling after him, "A stagecoach was held up not far outside of town. It was on its way from the territorial seat in Bannack with some fellows from the land title office. They were carrying a fair amount of cash!"

"The stage!" Martin exclaimed, turning back at the top of the stairs. "But who?"

Thaddeus shook his head angrily. "Outlaws from farther west in the territory. Men who couldn't find gold on their own and decided to steal it. They held up the coach and scared the passengers half to death. Robbed them and then were fixing to shoot them all. Imagine that!" He glanced impatiently at his friend. "Come on, Martin, we've got to get down to Doc's office."

Martin frowned. "Dr. Melbourne? What for?"

Thaddeus gave him an impatient look. "Because a couple of folks got shot up. I told you those boys were looking for trouble!"

"Shot!" Martin gasped. This was a little more excitement than he had been prepared for. "My Lord, Thaddeus, who?"

Thaddeus looked even more distressed. "The driver—Bill Marley—and Jessie Forbes."

Kate felt the blood drain from her face, and she sat down quickly on the stairs, her head buzzing. She was dimly aware of her father rushing down the hall toward his bedroom, of her mother's frightened voice calling questions, of Thaddeus shouting something in the background about Jessie. She pulled herself up on the banister and waited for her head to stop swirling.

"Mr. Schroeder," she gasped, her voice shaking, "Mr. Schroeder…"

"Yes, Kate?" Thaddeus responded distractedly, pacing at the foot of the stairs.

"Jessie. How is Jessie?" Kate held tightly to the railing, fearing that she might scream.

Thaddeus looked uncomfortable. "I don't know, Kate. She rode into it, apparently, and tried to stop the holdup. The marshal and some other men headed out with a wagon not long ago to get her and Marley. They should be coming into town soon." He stopped as Martin brushed past Kate and down the stairs. Both men rushed out, slamming the door behind them.

She slumped against the wall, willing herself to think. In her mind's eye she saw Jessie—her blue eyes, her golden hair, her shy grin. Kate was not a stranger to death. In the arduous months of their journey west, she had seen accidents and illness claim the lives of men, women, and children. *But like this? Could the life of someone as gentle and kind as Jessie simply be snuffed out by men with no regard for law or morality?* For the first time, Kate understood that the bright new world she had discovered held evil, too, a darkness where death came quickly, without concern for goodness or justice.

"Oh, Lord," she whispered, truly afraid as she had never been in her life. "Not Jessie. Please."

Her fear was what finally galvanized her. She rushed to her room and hastily pulled off her nightclothes. As she searched in her dresser for undergarments, she uncovered the photograph of Jessie she had taken the day of the picnic and then tucked away for safekeeping.

"Oh!" she gasped, lifting it tenderly in both hands. She stared at the image, her eyes slowly filling with tears as she recalled Jessie's easy smile and the soft touch of her hand as they sat side by side under a cloudless sky that had held no hint of tragedy. The memory was so powerful she trembled.

"Kate!" Martha called from the doorway of her daughter's room. "Where are you going at this hour?"

Kate crushed the photograph to her breast protectively and said without turning, "There's been a holdup. I'm going into town to see what's happening."

"That's no place for you," Martha admonished, more concerned for Kate's safety than propriety. "There may be trouble."

Kate finally faced her. "I must do something," she said stubbornly. "I can't stay here not knowing."

A large crowd had gathered in the street, shifting and pulsating with a life of its own. Men stood on the steps in front of the marshal's office, waving rifles and shouting to others to form a posse. Men, women, and children milled about in front of the doctor's storefront office, craning for a view and talking excitedly all at once. Kate stood at the outskirts of the group, struggling to see, straining to hear any word of Jessie. With each second, her anxiety grew.

"Excuse me," she asked of a man nearby. "Is there any news?"

He shook his head. "None for sure. Somebody's dead, but ain't no one saying who." He turned away as a swell of voices signaled that something was about to happen.

Kate's head was pounding so painfully she was afraid she would faint. When she heard the rattle of wagon wheels on the rutted road, she began pushing her way through the crowd without thought for good manners or behavior. *I must see for myself or go mad!*

As she drew closer, she saw men lifting blanket-shrouded bodies out of the wagon bed and carrying them into one of the buildings. Her mind refused to register the horror of that image. Struggling her way to the side of the wagon, she looked in, her eyes growing wide with fear as her breath caught painfully in her chest.

Jessie lay unmoving on the rough wooden boards, blood matted in her hair, a long gash just below her hairline and an ugly dark hole in her shirt at the base of her left shoulder. Her chest and part of the blanket were soaked red. Her lips were white, and she was so still. So very still.

"Jessie," Kate whispered, an eternity of agony in her voice. "Oh no, Jessie."

Strangers reached in to gently lift Jessie from the wagon, and Kate heard her moan faintly. The sound twisted her heart and she bit her lip to stop a cry. The image of Jessie in pain was unbearable. Worse still was the terror that she would vanish into that small, grim dispensary and not come out alive.

"Let me get a look at her," an irritated voice commanded as a harried-looking middle-aged man shoved his way through the press of people. Kate recognized Dr. Melbourne. He looked under Jessie's shirt, shook his head worriedly, then surveyed the faces of the townspeople gathered around.

"I need one of you women to help me with her. She's got a bullet in her chest, and if we don't get it out, she's going to die. I can't have somebody fainting when I start digging, so make sure you can take it."

Going to die…going to die…going to die…

"No," Kate said, her plaintive cry lost in the din. Not knowing what she might do, but knowing she couldn't stand by and let Jessie slip away, she squeezed her way between two large men, intent on reaching the injured woman. "I can hel—"

"Let's get going then, Doc," a blond woman with striking green eyes said firmly as she stepped to the doctor's side. She looked quickly at Jessie's inert form, then met his gaze squarely. "She's strong, but she ain't made of iron."

The doctor nodded, his face determined. "C'mon, Mae. We've got some work to do."

As several men carried Jessie into the building behind the doctor and his impromptu nurse, Kate stood in the midst of the crowd, feeling helpless and terribly alone.

Kate sat motionless on the same bench where she had been sitting when she had first seen Jessie Forbes a little more than two months before. A lifetime ago, it seemed to her now.

As she watched the door to the doctor's office, hoping for some word, she realized that all she had wanted these last few weeks was to see Jessie again. As soon as Jessie had ridden out of town after the roundup, Kate had missed her. Every day, as she went about her business—learning about her new home and her new responsibilities, helping Millie at the school, taking the occasional family portrait for new friends and neighbors, even entertaining Ken Turner—she missed her.

She missed her easy smile and her gentle way of talking and the way she made Kate feel special. She missed looking at her in her dusty blue denim pants and work-dampened shirt and feeling her own heart race for no apparent reason. She missed the way the sound of Jessie's spurs jingling could make her stomach quiver in that oddly nice way. She missed the light touch of Jessie's fingers when they brushed over her hand and the warmth it started inside. She missed all of her.

As she waited, wondering, trying not to think of what Jessie might be suffering, Kate's mind was blank for long periods. Then suddenly, she would remember why she was waiting. Jessie was hurt. Her throat tightened and tears threatened to spill. Hours passed, but she had no real sense of the passage of time. The sun grew bright and hung high in the sky, casting a harsh, merciless light over the brown earth street. People passed by, some spoke to her, and she nodded automatically. Her gaze never wavered from the door across the street.

Some time in the morning, a group of men galloped wildly into town, dismounted in a cloud of dust, and clustered in a roiling pack in front of the doctor's office. A man Kate had seen with Jessie at the roundup bolted indoors while the others paced about outside. He returned a short time later and said something to the agitated men who crowded around. Whatever news he relayed seemed to temporarily satisfy them, because now they, too, sat on the stairs or leaned against the railings, smoking and waiting.

Kate struggled for a way to describe emotions for which she had no words. *What will I feel if I never see Jessie again?* Without fully understanding it, she knew there would be an emptiness inside of her that would never be filled. She felt connected to Jessie in some deep way that she had never before experienced. *This can't happen,* she thought over and over. *Not now. Not when I'm just beginning to see.*

Trying to imagine the unimaginable, she had drifted so far into that unbearable place of loss that it took her several seconds to realize that the door across the street had opened. The blond woman who had volunteered to help the doctor with Jessie was talking to the waiting men gathered outside. Kate gave a small cry and jumped to her feet. *That woman will know about Jessie!*

As the doctor's helper started slowly down the street, Kate hurried after her, gathering her skirts in both hands, lifting the hem higher than was proper so that it would not trip her. She couldn't be bothered about how she looked now.

As Kate drew near, the woman's exhaustion became apparent. Her golden hair had fallen from its pins, tumbling in disarray over her bare shoulders. Her emerald green dress, far too revealing for walking about in, was rumpled and stained. Kate registered, in a distracted way, that she was quite beautiful.

She extended a trembling hand and touched the woman's arm. "Excuse me. I'm sorry," she said, her voice wavering. "Can you tell me how Jessie is?"

Mae turned, her eyes bleak. "She's alive, barely."

Kate swayed, suddenly dizzy. "Oh, thank God!"

"God had nothing to do with it," Mae answered bitterly.

"Please," Kate persisted, fighting to clear her vision, "could you tell me…" Her voice trailed off as spots danced in front of her eyes. The turmoil of the day and the absence of any nourishment combined to make her light-headed.

"Here now," Mae exclaimed, grasping Kate's arm with a strong hand. She peered at Kate's pale face closely, wondering why she should be so upset. Too tired to deal with one more crisis, she said brusquely, "Right now, I need a drink, and from the looks of you, you could use one, too. Come with me."

She's alive! Kate allowed herself to be led down the street, scarcely noticing their destination. Relief washed through her, and all she could see was Jessie's face. Mae took her down an alley and through a side door into the saloon. When she pointed to a table in the rear of the deserted room, Kate sank down gratefully.

Trudging to the bar, Mae slumped onto a stool. She pushed her hair away from her face. "Frank, give me a tall whiskey. And a brandy."

Frank poured the drinks and looked at her cautiously. "You want me to get you something to eat, Mae? You look pretty done in."

She started to shake her head no and then caught sight of Kate's trembling figure. The girl looked like she might swoon any second. "Maybe a couple of sandwiches."

He nodded, then asked quietly, "Jessie gonna make it?"

She looked at him, a lifetime of sorrow written in her expression. "If there is any justice in this world, she will."

Taking the drinks from him, she crossed to where Kate was sitting and put the brandy into Kate's hands. "Drink this."

Kate looked at it uncomprehendingly, still not herself.

"Come on, now," Mae said, not unkindly. "Drink it. Then we'll talk." She took a stiff gulp of her own drink and welcomed the fiery trail it burned down her throat. The pain was much better than the hopelessness she had felt looking at Jessie lying naked, a great gaping tear in her chest, her blood running red onto Mae's hands. She closed her eyes and held the glass with rigid fingers.

Kate took a swallow. Her eyes widened and she coughed, half choking. Color flooded her face and she seemed to waken, as if from a dream. "Oh!"

"First time's the hardest." Mae touched her hand. It was cold. "Drink some more, honey."

Kate took another sip and gasped, but Mae was right. It was easier the second time. She straightened up a little and looked intently at Mae. Her mind was clear, although her stomach felt odd. "Would you tell me now, please?"

"It ain't a pretty story."

"I don't care. I want to know what happened to her."

Mae heard the steel in her voice and thought that maybe Kate was tougher than she first appeared. She had a feeling she might like this young woman under different circumstances. "Doc says the head injury was just a flesh wound and won't hurt her any in the long run." She grimaced, trying to dispel the image of him probing in Jessie's shoulder with cold metal instruments while she held Jessie down. *How could a person live after something like that was done to her?* She was only thankful that Jess didn't seem to have had any awareness of it, only moaning softly as the doc worked. "Her shoulder's pretty torn up, but he got the bullet out. It didn't do damage to any, uh, vital organs."

"And she'll be all right?" Kate persisted, watching Mae's face, looking for the truth.

"The big problem was all that blood she lost." Mae finished her drink at a swallow. "That's the Doc's worry. If she does all right through the night, she should get well."

"Then it's not over yet," Kate whispered softly, feeling something inside her grow hard and cold. "She'll be all right. I know she will."

Mae studied the set of Kate's jaw and the way her spine stiffened. *The girl's got spirit, all right,* she thought to herself. She walked to the bar and returned with a bottle, plunking it down between them.

"Let's have another drink, sweetie."

Kate smiled grimly and held out her hand. "My name is Kate Beecher, by the way."

"Figured it might be," Mae said dryly and took her slender hand.

The level in the whiskey bottle had dropped an inch or two when Kate spied the leader of the group of cowboys from the doctor's earlier heading their way. He dropped into a chair across from Mae, his face grim.

"Hello, Jed," Mae said in a surprisingly gentle tone.

"I want to thank you, Mae. For what you did for Jess." His voice was very soft for such a big man.

"No need to thank me—not when it's Jess." Mae turned to Kate. "This here is Jed Harper, Jessie's foreman. Jed, Miss Kate Beecher."

"Hello, Mr. Harper."

"Ma'am," he said absently without taking his eyes from Mae. Anger hardened his voice. "The damn doctor won't let me in there to see her, and he won't say no more than that she's alive. What's going on?"

"I don't know much more than you do, Jed. We're just waitin', too." Mae's expression darkened. "Did they catch those bastards yet?"

Kate was shocked at the undisguised hatred in Mae's voice, only to realize an instant later that she felt exactly the same way. Without even knowing who the bandits were, she wished them dead. They'd hurt Jessie, meant to kill her. They'd almost taken from Kate the most special person she'd ever known. *Hatred* was not too strong a word for what she felt toward those who had harmed Jessie.

"Did they catch them?" Kate echoed.

"Ain't but one to catch." Jed laughed humorlessly. "Jess got one herself, with both of them firing on her, too. And from the looks of things, she got a piece of the other fella before…before he got her." His voice trembled, and he averted his gaze for a few seconds. "I sure don't want nothin' to happen to that girl. I promised Tom I'd look after her, and…and…I think it's been more like her lookin' after me."

Mae put her hand on his shoulder and smiled a little. "You know how hardheaded Jess can be. I don't imagine she's going to leave things at the ranch up to you for long."

Jed's grateful glance bespoke his thanks. He took a deep breath, suddenly looking determined. "You know, I'd best get back out there and see to things, or she'll be madder'n a hornet when she gets home."

"I'd keep an eye on your men, too, " Mae suggested sagely. "Jess wouldn't want them doing anything crazy if they catch this fella."

"No need to worry about the boys," he growled, his eyes hard. "When we get him, I'll take care of him myself."

Mae regarded him solemnly. "Be careful."

He thanked Mae and nodded courteously to Kate before striding out the door.

"Would he? Kill the man?" Kate asked.

"Probably," Mae said. *And everyone in town would thank him.*

Kate was silent for a long moment. Then she said with quiet conviction, "If I had a gun, I'd be ready to do it, too."

"Might not be a bad idea, even if you're not fixing to shoot someone." At Kate's puzzled glance, she added, "Learning how to shoot, I mean."

The thought had never crossed Kate's mind, although she had admired Jessie's apparent ability to protect herself. Maybe she would consider it. She examined Mae's face carefully, realizing for the first time how truly drawn and tired she looked. The woman had been everyone's strength all day.

"Mae," she said kindly, "why don't you go and get some rest. I'll wait here for any news."

"Lord, girl!" Mae gaped at her, unable to believe her ears. "Do you know where you are? And who *I* am, for that matter? Your folks'll take a fit when they hear where you spent the afternoon. You can't stay here!"

Kate placed her hand gently on Mae's and looked resolutely into her eyes. "You helped save Jessie's life—that's what I know about you. And so far, this place suits me fine. Just fine. I'm not going anywhere until we know."

Stubborn as well as pretty. Mae sighed, about to protest further.

Kate pressed her case. "Please let me do something. I can't sit at home and talk about foolishness. Please."

"All right, honey." Mae gave in to her tiredness. "But you stay back here, away from the bar. The boys are gonna be mean tonight, and I don't want you hearing all that bad talk."

Kate's eyes blazed, and she said bitterly, "Do you think words could bother me after seeing Jessie like that this morning?"

"No, I guess hard words can't hurt you none." Mae understood just what Kate was feeling, because she felt the same way. She wondered, however, if Kate knew what it meant.

CHAPTER ELEVEN

M ae awakened to an insistent rapping on her door.
"Mae, Mae, wake up! Mae!"

She sat up, pulling the ties of her bodice together hastily. "Come in, Kate. I'm awake."

Kate almost fell in, her face flushed. "The doctor sent word for you to come."

"What time is it?" Mae asked as she hurried about the room, gathering her things and pushing her hair into some kind of order.

"A little before ten."

Mae stared at her. "Lord! Your parents will have the marshal out searching for you."

"No, they won't," Kate declared. "I know my father won't go home until there's word from the posse about the outlaws, so I sent John Emory to tell my mother I was staying with him at the news office."

"There'll be the devil to pay for that tale," Mae said admiringly.

"That may be, but I don't care." Kate held the door open, too anxious to talk any more. "Hurry!"

They rushed down the hall, the sound of the dance-hall piano and loud male voices echoing up the stairwell from the bar below. Behind the closed doors on either side of the narrow corridor, muted laughter and low moans filtered through the thin walls. On any previous day of her life, Kate would have been shocked to hear what was happening in those rooms. But now, after coming face to face with the wickedness some men visited upon others and her own primitive instinct for retribution, she doubted that anything as simple as human passion would ever distress her again.

They left through the second-floor door to the stairs into the alley, the same way Kate had come with Jessie their first afternoon together. The streets were strangely empty; many of the men were still out riding with the marshal's posse. As they passed the newspaper office, Martin Beecher stepped out and halted in surprise at the sight of his daughter.

"Kate! What are you doing in town this late?"

"I'm on my way to the doctor's," she explained. "I'll be home later."

He stared, open-mouthed, as the two women barely slowed.

"But Kate," he protested faintly. "Without an escort..."

"Don't worry, Father. I'm fine."

"Wait for me there," he called after them. "I'll take you home."

Mae chuckled. "I'm guessing you're the only girl child in your house."

"The only child. Why?" Kate was breathless from their hurried pace, and decided then and there that she was going to abandon the tight corsets she had no need of under her simple daywear.

"Your father seems to lack practice with setting you to rights."

"I," Kate said with affected archness, "have never given him cause to."

"Never took his hand to you, either, I'll wager."

"No, never," Kate replied, suddenly serious. She wondered if that was what had driven Mae to the life she led—a father's harshness. It was impolite to inquire, and yet after the hours they had spent together, she felt they were friends. "Mae—"

"Things look awful quiet at the doc's."

Kate realized they had reached their destination, and she stared at the darkened storefront office, her eyes suddenly wide and frightened. "What do you think it means. What if Jessie—"

Mae's mouth was set in a grim line as she took Kate's hand. "Come on, honey. Let's go in."

Together they entered the small anteroom. The doctor, looking worn out and rumpled, slumped behind a scarred wooden desk. His face was barely visible in the faint light coming from an adjoining room.

"Well, Doc?" Mae asked. "She still with us?"

Kate held her breath, waiting for his words like a sentence of judgment.

"She's weak, but she's holding on better than I expected."

Kate's limbs suddenly refused to support her. With a little gasp, she sank onto one of the hard, straight-backed chairs that lined the wall opposite the doctor.

"It'll be a few days before she's likely to come around for more than a few minutes," Dr. Melbourne said, "and the wound'll need careful tending."

"I'll do that," Mae said instantly.

"Good. She's not well enough to move tonight, but tomorrow I think we ought to get her over to your place. It'll make lookin' after her easier."

"Won't be the first time we've turned a room upstairs into a sickroom."

He nodded as he recalled all the times that Mae had quietly provided a bed, food, and care to some unfortunate with nowhere else to go and received precious little thanks for it, too. He had always thought she was a damn fine woman. Too bad some of the good townspeople didn't agree.

"Doctor," Kate asked, "may I see her, please?"

The doctor looked startled, as if he'd forgotten Kate was there. "She's not awake yet, my dear. She wouldn't know you were there."

"I don't care about that," Kate insisted. "Just for a moment. Please."

Mae thought of how Kate had waited all day, pale and patient and determined. Knowing she'd probably regret it, she said, "Can't do no harm, can it, Doc?"

He looked from one to the other, and each regarded him steadily, their eyes never wavering. *Strange pair, a young society lady and a lady of the evening.* But he'd seen stranger things out here in this godless country, many of them far worse. He decided that he was no match for the two determined ladies.

"Not more than a minute," he relented. "And don't wake her."

An oil lamp, turned down low and situated in one corner, cast flickering shadows throughout the small windowless room. A single iron bed occupied the center of the narrow space, a straight-backed wooden chair nearby. The sound of low, raspy breathing broke the deep silence. As her eyes adjusted, Kate made out the still shape of Jessie's body beneath the covers. She pulled her lower lip hard between her teeth to stop its trembling and quietly stepped to the side of the bed.

Jessie's eyes were closed, her face pale and impossibly defenseless. A bandage covered the right side of her head, and the sight of a bright spot of blood in its center tore at Kate's heart. She was reminded that Jessie, for all her strength, was vulnerable, too. She watched the slow rise of her chest beneath the thin blanket. *How quickly life can change. Forever. Oh God.*

"Jessie," she whispered and softly stroked Jessie's cheek. "It's Kate. I don't know if you can hear me, but you're going to be all right. The doctor says so." She lifted Jessie's cool fingers and cradled them in her hand, stroking the work-roughened palm gently. "You must sleep, and get well."

Jessie didn't move, and Kate ached to gather her close. She wanted to *make* her well; she wanted to give Jessie her strength and shield her while she healed. She wanted that so desperately she hurt inside. Her throat tightened with a longing so intense she had to close her eyes against the pain, drawing some small comfort from the steady sound of Jessie breathing. Finally, needing to touch her just for an instant, she leaned forward and brushed her lips gently over Jessie's cheek. "Rest now," she whispered.

When she returned to the other room, she said to the doctor, "I'd like to help Mae look after her. Mae can't possibly do it all herself."

"Well, I think that's a fine idea, if Mae's willing to teach you some of what needs to be done."

Mae's first impulse was to refuse. The idea of sharing Jessie's care seemed a whole lot like sharing Jessie herself, and she wasn't entirely comfortable with that where Kate Beecher was concerned. She couldn't say just why, except that maybe it had to do with the way Kate looked when she spoke Jessie's name. All tender and fierce at the same time. Kate had that look now. Mae sighed. "I don't think I could keep you away, could I?"

"No, Mae. You couldn't."

"Figured that. You come round in the morning, then," Mae said. Some things would have to be settled later.

❖

"Martin, you must forbid it," Martha Beecher declared in an agitated voice after Kate had made her announcement and gone up to bed. "You simply have to make her see reason. It is just not fitting for her to be spending time in that…that place. And with those women! She has to think of her reputation!"

Martin frowned. "For heaven's sake, Martha, she wants to help take care of a woman who was…uh, injured…saving people's lives." He thought it best not to remind his wife that Jessie Forbes had been shot. Martha was already distraught enough. "No one is going to think anything evil about Kate for that."

Martha was hurt by her husband's harsh tone and tears came to her eyes. "I'm only thinking of Kate."

"I know you are, dear." He went to his wife and put his hands on her shoulders. "But you must try to understand. Life is hard, and women out here need to be different. All of us must do things we never had to do before. Kate understands that. She is doing the proper thing."

She looked at him, clearly unconvinced. "What she *needs* is to be settled and safe. I'm not at all sure that this place is good for her. Not sure at all."

"Kate is only doing the charitable thing," Martin soothed. "It's how we've raised her to behave, and I'm sure she'll be just fine. As to the other—well, now, you've said yourself that you like Ken Turner. She'll be settled soon enough, I imagine."

Martha rested her head on his shoulder, her anger replaced by worry. "Oh, Martin, she seems to have changed since we came here. I feel as if I hardly know her."

He smoothed her hair, holding her carefully. "Kate is a good child. Let's give her a little time, and if you still feel she's not on the proper course, we'll talk about what needs to be done. I'm sure that you know what's best for her."

She nodded, wishing fervently that Kate had stayed behind in Boston, where women knew what to expect of life and what was expected of them in return. She could see only disappointment ahead if Kate continued her increasingly independent ways, because even on this wild frontier, there was no future in such thoughts for a woman.

CHAPTER TWELVE

For a long time, there was a horrible pain tearing away inside her, and when it surged, her mind retreated. She slept. While she slept, she dreamed. She wandered over vast barren prairies and through dark mountain passes, searching for a place to rest. Each time she stopped, she waited, lonely and so cold, for the comfort that never came.

She drifted in and out of consciousness, dimly aware that she was not alone. Soft voices soothed her, and softer hands placed cool cloths on her burning forehead, bathing the fever from her skin. Gentle, insistent hands held her and forced nourishment between her lips. She struggled less and less with each touch, letting herself be healed. Her body ached everywhere, but the worst assault was the burning pain in her shoulder. Eventually it dampened to a dull throb. In the end, hunger overpowered the pain, and she awoke.

Her first thought was that she didn't know where she was. And she didn't know why she hurt. She tensed, uncertain and afraid, and the small movement made her chest throb. She heard familiar sounds—horses clomping, men's voices, the tinkle of dance-hall music. A gentle breeze touched her cheek, and she smelled cattle and the vaguely familiar scent of a woman's perfume. Opening her eyes, Jessie carefully turned her face slowly in the direction of the raised window. She blinked against the first assault of sunlight, even as she welcomed the banishment of the dark that had surrounded her for so long. The plain cotton curtains fluttered around the woman who sat before the window, a book open in her lap.

Kate.

The knot of tension in her stomach loosened, and Jessie lay silent for a moment, studying her. She didn't appear to be reading but stared down into the street, her expression distant. Wisps of black hair, too thick to be contained by the fine net that held the coil of shining curls at her nape, escaped to frame her face. Her full lips were unsmiling, and there were dark smudges under her eyes. She looked worn and weary, older than Jessie remembered. Even though she was clearly exhausted, Jessie still thought her beautiful.

"How long have you been here?" she asked.

Kate gave a startled cry and spun away from the window, her eyes wide. What she saw was what she had prayed for, every moment of the endless days since the wagon had carried Jessie into town—Jessie, her deep blue eyes clear and strong; Jessie, perfect lips curled into a faint smile of greeting. *Jessie.* The resolve that had sustained Kate through near sleepless nights and days of worry dissolved with the swift rush of relief, and tears sprang to her eyes. She whispered Jessie's name, holding herself tightly, and cried.

"Hey, hey now," Jessie whispered, aching to comfort her. She felt so weak she doubted she could get out of bed, let alone walk that far. Still, the sight of Kate's unhappiness motivated her to try. She made one ineffectual attempt to sit up but quickly abandoned the idea when a searing pain ran down her arm. She gritted her teeth for a moment, then said, "Don't cry, Kate."

Swiping at the tears on her cheek with both palms, Kate hurried to Jessie's side, smiling tremulously. "Don't try to get up. You've been… shot, Jessie." Just saying the words caused her stomach to clench with a fresh surge of anxiety and fear.

"Don't worry," Jessie gasped, watching the concern flicker across Kate's face. "I'll save getting out of bed for a bit later."

Kate touched Jessie's hand, stroking it softly. "What you need to do is sleep."

"That's all I've *been* doing, seems like," Jessie protested feebly. Threading her fingers through Kate's, she tried a valiant smile. The throbbing in her shoulder made it hard for her to think clearly, and she closed her eyes against the pain. Kate's fingers were so warm, and her touch seemed to soothe the hurt places inside. "If you could just stay another minute…"

"I can stay as long as you need me," Kate whispered.

As she watched Jessie drift off, she pondered the strength of the attachment she felt for her, so very different than any she held for her girl friends, here or in the East. She cared for her friends—why she'd come to love Millie in the weeks she'd known her. She enjoyed sharing her secrets and hopes with her new friend, and vice versa, but Millie didn't haunt her thoughts and dreams the way Jessie did. And she never got that floating feeling when she looked into Millie's eyes. The most telling truth, however, was knowing that as much as she would suffer if anything ever happened to Millie, her heart wouldn't break the way it nearly had when she'd almost lost Jessie. No, Jessie was special in a way no one ever had been before, and Kate was at a loss to explain those feelings.

What have you done to me, Jessie Forbes?

"Kate?"

"I'm here."

Jessie sighed, instantly calmed by the sound of Kate's voice. When she opened her eyes, she discovered Kate still close by in the chair she had pulled up to the bedside. It was dark outside the window now.

"Same day?" Jessie asked.

"Yes." Kate smiled and offered Jessie some water, supporting her head with a hand behind Jessie's neck while she sipped. "Feeling better?"

"Some," Jessie acknowledged, grateful for even the temporary cessation of the worst of the ache. "What happened? And I know I've been shot. You don't need to tell me that."

"What can you remember?"

"Not much." Jessie frowned. "The last thing I clearly recall is leaving Mae's about sunup."

"Oh?" Kate asked. Mae hadn't mentioned *that.* She pushed aside the quick surge of hurt that Jessie had been in town and hadn't come to visit her. But then, she'd made no attempt to see Jessie either. *That will have to change.*

"Something wrong?" Jessie asked, noting Kate's frown.

"No. Nothing." Kate took a breath and smiled. "You're better, and that's what matters."

"So tell me what trouble I ran into."

As Kate explained about the stagecoach robbery, Jessie narrowed her eyes, nodding now and then. "I remember some of that—thought I'd dreamed it."

"I imagine it will all come back to you as you heal."

"What about those bastards that held up the stage? Did I at least get one of 'em, do you know?"

"Yes," Kate replied, wondering how Jessie could be so calm about having been involved in a gunfight, and having been shot, and possibly having killed a person. She wondered also at herself, discussing something she had never even imagined before as if it were a common occurrence. But then, perhaps it shouldn't really seem so strange. During the torturous hours of waiting, not knowing if Jessie would recover, she had come to realize that she was a far different woman now than the sheltered young girl of less than a year ago. She had found an inner strength she might never have known had she not come to this wild and dangerous place, had she not met this fierce yet so gentle woman. "You saved lives, Jessie. I'm so proud of you."

"No," Jessie said quickly, blushing at the praise. "Anyone would have done the same. I just happened to be there."

Kate smiled at her clear discomfort. "You say that, but I don't think so."

"You look tired," Jessie remarked, hoping to change the subject but also concerned about the shadows under the other woman's eyes.

"Oh, I must look a fright!" Kate brushed her hair back, suddenly self-conscious. But the heavy locks would not be tamed.

"No," Jessie said seriously. "You're beautiful."

Kate colored slightly, but her eyes shone with pleasure. She asked tenderly, "Are you in pain?"

Jessie forced a grin. "Not as bad as the time the bull ran me down when I was ten." She held Kate's eyes for a long moment, marveling at their dark beauty, and quickly forgot the throbbing in her shoulder. Looking at Kate was a tonic all of its own. "How long have I been here?"

"Almost a week." *It seemed forever*, Kate thought.

During that week, she and Mae had taken turns sitting by Jessie's bed, changing her nightshirt when she soaked it through with sweat, replacing the bloody bandages and cleaning the terrible wounds, forcing her to drink, and soothing her when she had cried out in the throes of some dream terror. Several of Mae's girls took over at times to give them a break, but Kate had come every day, despite her mother's increasingly vocal objections. She usually sent the others away, preferring to look after Jessie herself. All except Mae.

Mae would often come in when Kate was there, simply to stand at the foot of the bed and watch Jessie sleep. When she was satisfied that Jessie was all right, she would disappear into the night. Where she went and what she did were none of Kate's affair, although Kate was fairly sure she knew precisely what Mae was doing. Oddly, she found that she didn't care. Jessie had almost been killed. If it hadn't been a gunshot, it might have been a stampeding horse or a rockslide up in the hills. Realizing that, Kate suddenly had a new appreciation of what truly mattered in life, and it certainly wasn't judging what someone else did to survive.

"The doctor says you'll be fine, but you need to rest," she told Jessie.

"Damn, I feel weak as a kitten." Jessie grimaced. "And I'm not going to get any stronger laying up here." She tried again to push herself up. A wave of dizziness rolled over her, followed quickly by a fierce rush of pain. She groaned and struggled not to surrender to the dark curtain that crept over her vision.

"Oh!" Kate reached for her without thinking, supporting Jessie's shivering body against her side with a protective arm around her shoulders. Holding Jessie's face to her breast, she stroked the damp hair back from her forehead. Jessie trembled. Kate caught her breath as her insides made a little dip. She had never been this close to another human being before, other than her parents. Nothing she had ever imagined had prepared her for the wave of tenderness that swept through her. She could scarcely breathe. With effort, she said quietly, "You can't get up. Not just yet."

"Don't want to now," Jessie mumbled. Too weak to protest and not wanting to move even if she had been strong enough, she relaxed into the soft embrace. It felt so good to close her eyes and feel Kate stroke her face.

"Well," Mae said acerbically from the doorway behind them. "I guess our patient's getting better." She carried a tray to the dresser before turning to the women on the bed. *They're looking mighty cozy.*

Kate eased Jessie gently back onto the pillow and rose from her chair, making room by the bedside for Mae. She met Mae's eyes squarely but could not read the expression in her cool green gaze. When Mae looked from her to Jessie, her face softened.

"How are you, Montana?" she asked huskily. "It sure is good to see you with your eyes open."

Jessie worked up a smile. "I'm downright embarrassed, Mae. Letting a couple of no-goods get the best of me and causing all this trouble."

"Jess, the only trouble you would have caused is if you'd up and died on us!" Mae gestured toward the dresser. "Brought you some soup and whatnot."

"I'm sorry, but I can't seem to stay awake." Jessie grinned a little sheepishly. "I'm hungry enough, but I think it'll have to keep a bit." She didn't want to admit that the pain was growing the longer she stayed awake.

With a hint of challenge in her eyes, Mae turned to Kate. "I suspect Jess needs some peace and quiet."

"Yes." Kate couldn't bear the thought of leaving, but Mae looked ready to argue, and that would only upset Jessie. "I think we should *both* go and let her rest."

"Seems like," Mae said. "You sleep then, Montana."

After the briefest hesitation, Kate headed for the door, holding it open until Mae passed through. With a last look in Jessie's direction, she closed it gently.

Jessie awakened the following day to discover that the sun was already high in the sky and she had lost nearly another day. She didn't mind so much when she found that she was not alone.

"What is that you're reading, Kate?" she asked, managing to sit up this time with much less pain.

"The sonnets of Mr. William Shakespeare." Kate placed her finger on the page and lightly closed the cover on the leather-bound book. She was heartened to see how much better Jessie appeared. There was color in her face and a sparkle in her eyes that Kate had feared she might never see again. "Do you know them?"

"I've heard of *him*, but I'm not much for poetry. I'd rather have a story, I guess."

Kate smiled. "Every time I read one of his sonnets, I find something new to enjoy, even though I know most of them by heart."

Contemplating Kate's words, Jessie ventured, "Like always being surprised at how pretty the sunset is, even after seeing a thousand of them."

"Yes." Kate lifted her eyes to Jessie's. Her expression was full of tenderness. "Exactly like that."

Jessie flushed, having never known such quiet communion in the rough world of cowboys. For some unknown reason, it did funny things to her breathing, and it wasn't from something broken, but from something right.

Kate's hands trembled as they held tightly to the thin volume in her lap. Jessie saw her as no one else ever had. To others, she had always been just another young woman with her future predetermined by virtue of her sex and status. Her father had allowed her to be different from other young girls, but only to a point. She might read in the college library, but he had not suggested she attend classes there. Jessie seemed content to let her simply be. The silence grew heavy as their eyes held, two women united not by common experience but by a common sensitivity that drew them together more surely than convention or class.

"It makes me feel better," Jessie said quietly, "you being here."

"I'm glad. It makes me feel better, too."

Jessie blushed, uncertain why the way Kate sounded, her voice all warm and soft, made her stomach jumpy. She struggled for some kind of conversation, when she mostly just wanted to look at Kate. "What have you been doing, since I saw you at the roundup?"

Kate told her about her part-time teaching and the photographs she'd made of the dozen youngsters at the school.

"I bet that's something to see."

Jessie's voice held a note of pride, and Kate flushed at the praise. "The children loved it. And now a few of the parents want me to make family photographs for them."

"That's a real gift," Jessie said. "Was that what you were studying on being back in Boston? A…photographer?"

"Oh no," Kate said with a surprised laugh. "It was…is…just a hobby."

"Seems like more than that," Jessie commented. "So what *were* your plans?"

"I…" Kate frowned, aware that she had no answer because she'd never thought the future was hers to plan. "I hadn't decided."

"Well, I guess you could do most anything you wanted."

The idea was so new that Kate had trouble grasping it, but excitement swelled in her breast. "I could, couldn't I."

Jessie's lids fluttered closed but she managed to mumble, "Sure."

Kate smiled and returned to her book of poems. She'd read the sonnets many times before, but today for some reason, the passionate words of love resonated in her heart in a way they never had before.

CHAPTER THIRTEEN

Jessie pulled the window curtain aside and looked down the street for the sixth time in as many minutes. It was well past the time that Kate usually arrived in the morning, and she was starting to worry. It was only a mile or so from Kate's home into town, and almost the entire route was well populated, but still, she was a woman out alone. Ordinarily, Jessie wouldn't have been so anxious, but her nerves were jangling as she considered what she was about to do.

"Well, you're up and dressed awfully early," a voice behind her observed.

Jessie turned. Mae stood just inside the door, still in her dressing gown.

"I want to go home," Jessie said without preamble.

"Now Jess, the doc said you couldn't ride yet." Mae worked to keep her voice even "You know darn well if you go back to the Rising Star that's the first thing you'll want to do."

Jessie leaned against the window and muttered under her breath. Her face was thinner, but her color had returned. "Mae, I just can't stand it anymore. Lord knows what's going on out there. Jed is a good man, and I know it. But that's *my* ranch!" She paced a few impatient steps. It still hurt to move, but sitting still was making her crazy. "I just won't be right until I get out into the air again—out of town."

"It won't be much longer." *Lord, you can't tell these cowboys anything!* "If you open up that tear in your shoulder, you could be in real trouble."

"Mae, I swear!" Jessie pushed her hands into the pockets of her pants. "I just don't feel healthy in here. And as kind as you've been, I feel like I'm fettered."

Laughing, Mae went to her and lightly gripped her tense shoulders, taking care to avoid the area of her wound. She had to stand on tiptoe to look into those blue eyes, and she leaned lightly against Jessie for support. Smiling at the perplexed expression in Jessie's eyes, she said, "Oh, I know you're grateful, Montana. And I know just what you're feeling. I've known a lot of cowboys in my time, and I learned better than to try to tame one. But if you go, you'd better promise to look after yourself. You ain't seen nothing 'til you've seen me mad."

"I *have* seen you mad, and believe me, I don't want to chance it. It's my shoulder that's ailing, not my head!" Jessie smiled down at Mae and gently encircled her waist. "I want to thank you, Mae, for everything you've done for me. I know how bad off I was, and I owe you my life, I guess."

"I had help," Mae acknowledged. Tilting her head back, she searched Jessie's face and said softly, "Something special would have gone out of my life if I lost you, Jess." She pressed closer, sliding her arms around Jessie's neck. Gently she brushed Jessie's mouth with her lips. She'd meant it innocently enough, but the feel of their bodies together brought a low moan from Mae's throat. Her fingers slipped into the thick hair at Jessie's nape as she came dangerously close to kissing her like she'd always wanted to.

"Oh, my!" Kate cried as she stood in the doorway taking in the scene. She stared, speechless, at Jessie holding Mae in her arms.

Wordlessly, Jessie looked over at Kate as she gently released Mae. The kiss had taken her by surprise, the softness of Mae's lips calling up memories. That night in the bath, she had dreamed of kissing lips as soft as those, but not Mae's. With a flutter of relief, she said, "Why, Kate! Come in."

"I'm sorry. I should have knocked," Kate said coolly. Her first flush of embarrassment at coming upon such an intimate scene was quickly replaced by something else. She wasn't sure why, but the sight of Mae in Jessie's arms made her angry. Rapidly, she composed herself, hoping neither woman would notice her trembling hands.

Jessie smiled, innocently pleased to see her at last, the kiss already forgotten. "I've been wondering where you were."

Confused, Kate stared from one to the other of them, chiding herself for making too much of what she had just witnessed. Jessie's greeting to her was warm and welcoming, the way it always was. But a feeling of disquiet still lingered. Her heart pounding, trying to appear unperturbed, she answered, "Hello, Jessie. Hi, Mae."

Mae stepped slowly away from Jessie and gave Kate an enigmatic smile. "Yes, Kate. Do come in. I was just...uh, saying goodbye to Montana here."

"Goodbye!" Kate cried with dismay. She had consciously avoided thinking about the inevitable. She had always known Jessie would leave once she was healed. Then, Kate feared, she would be left as she had been before, alone in a life she found increasingly oppressive. Her heart sinking, she repeated softly, "Goodbye."

Mae touched Jessie lightly on the arm as she headed for the door. "Don't forget to come calling now, Jess."

"You know I won't forget. And thanks," Jessie said.

Kate barely gave Mae a nod as she passed, glaring instead at Jessie, who was awkwardly trying to strap on her gun belt without using her injured arm. Fear and sadness made her tone sharper than she intended. "Just what are you doing?"

"I'm going home, Kate."

"It's too soon." Kate placed the parcel of books and the basket of food she carried on the dresser. Struggling not to raise her voice, she said, "You'll hurt yourself."

Jessie held up a hand when she saw the frown on Kate's face. "Now don't you go at me, too. Jed is coming in the buckboard so I won't have to ride. I've already promised I'll be careful."

"You haven't been out of bed but for a day. Here, let me do that." Kate reached around Jessie's waist with both arms to settle the wide holster on Jessie's narrow hips. Moving closer, she fed the worn tongue through the silver buckle, fumbling slightly with the clasp.

Jessie went very still as Kate worked, acutely aware of Kate's fingers brushing over her legs. Kate's hair smelled fresh, like flower petals ripe with spring pollen.

"I promise to lie low when I get there," she said. "But I need to get going."

"How does this thing tie?" Kate's head remained bent as she studied the thong hanging from the holster.

"Around my leg," Jessie answered a bit hoarsely. She was starting to shake, but she didn't feel ill. She stiffened as Kate's hands encircled her thigh. She felt again as she had in the dream, jumpy and churning deep inside. The intimacy of it was frightening and exhilarating all at once.

"Oh," she murmured in surprise as swift heat hit her in the stomach. Suddenly unsteady, she placed her good hand on Kate's shoulder to keep her balance. "Kate," she breathed uncertainly. *Lord, what's happening?*

Kate straightened quickly, sliding both hands to her hips. Jessie's arms came around her waist. They stood, a whisper apart, while the room and reality receded, leaving only the two of them in a place out of time. Jessie leaned her forehead to Kate's and closed her eyes, content to rest. Kate eased her hands to Jessie's back and rubbed gently up and down, liking the hard strength of her. Somewhere out in the hall a woman laughed.

"You're not well yet, " Kate whispered, her lips close to Jessie's cheek. She felt their bodies touch, all along her front, and the room became unbearably warm.

"I know," Jessie conceded, her voice trembling. "But I will be, Kate. I promise."

Kate wanted to forget that Jessie was leaving, longed to forget that Jessie could be hurt again. She wanted only to be close to her, to feel her heart beat and to smell the clean, fresh fragrance of her skin. But she couldn't forget the image of Jessie lying in that wagon, so still, so pale. She sighed, half in anger and half in exasperation, and leaned back in the circle of Jessie's arms, probing those astonishing blue eyes. When she saw that the decision was made, she took a step back, breaking their embrace. "Jessie Forbes, you are the most stubborn woman I have ever met."

"Thank you," Jessie said, a grin flickering at the corner of her mouth. Now that there was distance between them, her head began to clear, and she crossed to the side of the bed where her valise stood open.

"It's not funny," Kate snapped, but she couldn't look at her and hold on to her anger. She thought Jessie had never been more attractive than she was now, leaning against the bedpost, her arms folded across her chest, one leg crossed in front of the other, all leather and worn denim and cocksureness. Kate felt her face grow hot, and she knew

Jessie saw it.

Jessie recognized the lingering blaze of anger in Kate's eyes, but she saw the worry there, too. Seriously, she asked, "What is it, Kate? Have I done something to upset you?"

"I just can't bear to see you hurt again," Kate confessed, tears unexpectedly close to the surface. The days and nights of worry were still too fresh in her mind. "Will you be careful, Jessie? Please?"

"Of course." Jessie closed the satchel and lifted it in her right hand, wishing she could erase the unhappiness that still clouded Kate's face. She realized, quite suddenly, that she didn't want to say goodbye. The best thing about being here in town had been seeing Kate every day and spending peaceful hours just quietly talking with her. For the first time, it occurred to her how lonely the ranch would be now.

"Come visit, Kate," she said. "Come out to the ranch one day soon."

"You did promise me a tour." The glow Jessie's suggestion had brought to her eyes disappeared just as quickly. "But it's an hour's ride away, isn't it?"

"Less on a good horse, but you'll need a buckboard. You can have John Emory bring you around. He's always itching to spend time with Jed and the boys. I don't imagine he'd need much prompting."

Kate felt certain her parents would not object to John Emory taking her out for a drive. "This week?"

"Yes, soon as you can." Jessie walked to the door and, as an afterthought, added, "Will you do something for me, Kate?"

Kate waited breathlessly, feeling in that moment that Jessie could ask her anything and she would agree. "You know I will, Jessie."

"It's Mae."

"Mae?" Kate echoed, not understanding.

"You're the only friend, besides me, that Mae really has in this town. The saloon girls look to her for help more often than the other way around, and I expect it gets hard for her…and lonely. I don't get by nearly enough with all I have to do out at the ranch. Will you look in on her now and then?"

"Of course I will," Kate promised, but she felt a pang of unease. Were she and Mae friends? She was no longer sure.

Chapter Fourteen

Jessie sat on her front porch, her boots up on the rail, oiling the stock of her rifle with more vigor than it required. Across the yard, Jed and several of the men were cutting tree lengths for fence posts. She watched them work, feeling useless and out of sorts, muttering colorfully to herself about foremen who didn't have an ounce of respect.

Jed had finally lost his temper after the third time he had to take the saw away from her and told her he was sorry he ever went to pick her up. "Would've left you there in that damn hotel, if I'd'a known you'd be this much trouble to have around," he had complained. "You won't be worth nothing the rest of the year if you don't let that shoulder heal. And I don't plan on doin' your share of the work forever, so just let that damn saw be!"

She knew he was right, but after three days at home, she was chafing under the weight of inactivity. She had worked every day of her life in some capacity, with the exception of Sundays, when even nonbelievers took a few hours' rest. And there was work to be done now, but most of it required physical strength, which left her sitting on her porch or pacing a path outside the corrals, watching the hands work *her* horses.

Jessie saw the clouds of dust before she heard the clatter of wheels on the road to her house. On her feet in an instant, she leaned over the porch rail, straining to make out the driver and passenger. When she saw who it was, she bounded down the steps to meet the buckboard pulling up in her yard.

"Kate," she cried, striding alongside the wagon, gazing up at Kate. "You've come!"

"I said I would!" Kate called, holding her bonnet with one hand as John Emory slowed the team to a halt. She looked down from her perch on the high seat, almost too happy for words. Jessie's undisguised delight made her forget completely the struggle she'd had with her parents to get permission for John to take her about in the buckboard. To be entirely proper, the two of them should have been chaperoned, but even Martha acknowledged that no one in town would object to the Schroeder boy escorting Kate for her own safety. And since Kate insisted that she needed the buckboard to carry her camera while visiting some of her new friends who lived outside of town, her parents had agreed to the arrangement. It had taken very little convincing to get John to continue as far as Jessie's ranch after she'd spent an agitated hour with friends trying to make conversation.

"You look wonderful," Kate said, pleased to see the healthy color in Jessie's face. "How are you?"

Jessie grinned and extended both arms as Kate stepped onto the running board to climb down. She wasn't thinking about her shoulder. She didn't seem to be able to think of much of anything else beyond Kate when they were together. "I'm better now. Let me get you down from there."

Kate placed one hand on Jessie's right shoulder to steady herself, holding her skirt up with the other. "You can't lift me. Let John."

Slipping her right arm around Kate's waist, Jessie merely laughed and pulled Kate into her arms, supporting most of the smaller woman's weight on the side away from her injured shoulder. She held her for just a moment, surprised by Kate's firm suppleness. Then she gently released her. "I'm fine," she repeated, her eyes on Kate's flushed face. *I really do feel much better when you're near.*

John Emory jumped down and stood by the back of the wagon, hands stuffed in the pockets of his trousers, looking uncertain.

"Jed's over in the corral behind the main barn with some of the men," Jessie told him. "Why don't you go on over?"

"Sure thing, Jessie." He looked relieved. "I'll be back in a bit, Kate."

"Don't worry. I'm just fine." Kate waved vaguely in his direction as he hurried away, unable to take her eyes from Jessie, who wasn't wearing her usual workday vest and chaps. The pants and soft cotton shirt accentuated her slender body, and Kate knew very well what that body looked like under those clothes. She'd bathed her and helped dress her a dozen times when she'd been recovering. But for the first time she was thinking of her not as a patient but as a vital, attractive woman. Realizing that she was staring, she said shyly, "It's so good to see you."

"Yes." Jessie found it hard to do anything but look in return. Finally, she asked, "Would you like to walk around a little? See the ranch?"

"Oh, yes. Please." Kate slipped her hand through Jessie's arm, and, almost as an afterthought, added, "And I was hoping that you could teach me how to drive the buckboard, too."

Jessie stopped dead. "The buckboard?"

"I can't very well drag John Emory out here every time I want to come visiting, now can I?"

"You can't drive out here alone, either, especially unarmed," Jessie said with finality. She began walking again toward the horse barns as if the matter were settled.

"Well, I thought I'd save the shooting lessons until the next visit," Kate remarked with calm determination.

Jessie grinned. "We'll let your hands heal from the blisters you're gonna get handling that team before we start in with the Winchester."

"That's sounds quite reasonable."

Kate smiled an excited smile so brilliant that Jessie was momentarily lost. Regaining a little of her usual composure, she announced, "I'll show you the brood mares down at the corral, then we'll take the buckboard out to the north pasture where the yearlings are summering. Don't see why you can't drive out there."

When at length they returned to the shade of Jessie's porch, cool drinks in hand, Kate had seen most of the Rising Star ranch within easy riding distance of the house. She had also discovered that driving the buckboard was quite a bit easier than controlling the heavy wagon in which she and her family had traveled west. When her father had needed to lever the wagon's wheels from some mud-laden trench or to lead the horses by hand through a dangerous stretch, Kate had taken the reins. She had loved the excitement of handling the team then, and she loved the freedom that driving the buckboard would give her now.

"How are your hands?" Jessie inquired gently.

Kate pulled off her cotton gloves, which were streaked with grime. "Red and tender, but no blisters yet."

"Try this. Might take the sting out." Jessie handed Kate a tin of thick yellow salve that smelled surprisingly like honey.

Kate smeared the ointment over the sore spots on her palms. She could hide her ruined gloves, but she wouldn't want her mother to see blisters. She'd never be able to explain them without revealing her visit to the ranch, and that was something she wasn't ready to confide. Instinctively, she knew her mother would object, and she was determined that she would not allow anything to stand in the way of her friendship with Jessie.

She placed the tin on the rail and surveyed the slowly rising expanse of hills that climbed steeply toward the mountains edging the horizon. A stream flowed in a ribbon of blue across the golden brown flatland. The gently undulating plains were marked here and there by patches of greener grass and clusters of trees. "It's so peaceful here." She caught sight of Jessie's face in profile and thought how much Jessie was like her land, bold and strong and sure. "Beautiful."

Jessie nodded. "Yes."

"Do you ever get lonely?" Kate asked, wondering if perhaps she was the only one who longed for something more.

"Sometimes." Jessie met her questioning gaze and said quietly, "Sometimes I miss you."

Kate's lips parted in soft surprise. "I thought about you every day after the roundup. I so enjoyed being with you."

"Same here." Jessie moved close beside her at the rail, their shoulders gently touching. Her hand brushed Kate's where it curled on the flat board top. She lifted it carefully and turned the palm up to her view. "I'll have to get you heavier gloves. Those fancy ones of yours won't do for out here." Her expression changed to one of hope and uncertainty. "If you'll be coming out again soon."

"Oh yes, I want to." Kate drew a shaky breath. She seemed to be shaking everywhere, but not as if from illness. As if from a terrible happiness. "I *will*." She closed her fingers around Jessie's. "You promised to teach me to shoot."

"Did I?"

"You most certainly did," Kate asserted seriously, but her eyes danced with mischief.

Jessie laughed quietly, nearly giving in to the urge to touch Kate's hand to her cheek. Instead she tucked Kate's arm through hers and drew Kate close to her side. "Then I guess I will. Next time."

Next time. Kate smiled, feeling far, far less alone.

As each day passed, Jessie's strength returned. Her shoulder healed, and she could finally ride again. From sunup to sundown, she kept busy with the ever-present demands of the ranch, but when evening came, she stood on the porch surrounded by silence, feeling the disappointment of yet another day when Kate had not come. Sleep remained an elusive respite, and she grew weary in body and soul.

One morning, two weeks after Kate's visit, she decided to survey the creek where she meant to build a dam. There was a small hollow between two wooded knolls that would make a fine natural shelter for the animals to winter. All it needed was water. The day was warm, and she let Star have her head, riding low over her neck as they flew across the countryside. Nearing the hill overlooking the gully, she saw figures moving under the trees. Rustlers were not uncommon, so she approached slowly, one hand casually on her gun belt. When she was close enough to make out the intruders' faces, her jaw set in a hard, angry line and her insides turned cold.

Kate had watched the horse and rider gallop across the flatlands, and she knew long before she could see her face that it was Jessie. She couldn't mistake that lean figure and graceful seat on the thundering animal for anyone else. As Jessie drew closer, Kate saw her set expression, but took it for wary caution, thinking that Jessie had not yet recognized her. Ken Turner, lulled to sleep by the effects of a hearty picnic lunch and the warm sun, napped contentedly beside her on the broad cotton cloth she had spread out on the grass. She placed her hand gently on his shoulder and shook him as Jessie rode up to them.

"Jessie!" Kate was elated to see her. She had tried for days to convince her father to let her take the buckboard out alone, but all her arguing had been to no avail. She wanted desperately to visit Jessie again, but John Emory had been needed at the newspaper office and could not get free to accompany her.

To complete her frustration, she could no longer politely refuse Ken Turner's repeated invitations for an afternoon drive, especially when her mother kept urging her to accept. So finally she found herself in the only place she wanted to be—on the Rising Star ranch—with precisely the wrong person. It had been agony sitting for hours with Ken Turner, making casual conversation and feigning interest in the attorney's self-important plans, while all the time her mind was on Jessie. *And now she's here.*

"Hello, Kate," Jessie said from astride her mount.

"It's so good to see you," Kate said. "Mr. Turner and I were just having lunch. Come join us."

"No. No thank you, Kate." Jessie's voice was tight as she looked at the man slowly sitting up. Her glance quickly surveyed the picnic basket and Kate's hand on Ken's shoulder, and she flushed. "I'm sorry, I didn't mean to bother you. I didn't know who you were at first."

Ken, awake now, smiled in a rather superior way. "Oh, not at all, Miss Forbes. After all, we are trespassing, so to speak." He slipped his arm possessively around Kate's waist, looking for all the world like a man content with himself, and posturing as if Kate were already his.

Jessie stared at him coldly. "Kate is always welcome on my land. I think she knows that."

"We're still taking advantage of your hospitality. I'm sure Kate would enjoy a little cha—"

"I've business to see to," Jessie said curtly. She disliked him intensely, with his smug arrogance and the way he handled Kate. *Handled her.* Like she was his already. Jessie's vision narrowed as if she were sighting down the barrel of her Winchester, and Ken Turner's face filled her view. "I'll be going."

Kate had never heard such harsh tones from Jessie before, nor seen such icy fury in her face. She didn't understand why she was so angry, and she'd missed her so. "Wait. Jessie. I was hoping to see you."

"I wouldn't want to interrupt your afternoon, Miss Beecher."

Gazing into her impenetrable blue eyes, Kate slid out of Ken's grip and rose clumsily to her feet, almost falling over her crinoline in her haste. "But it's you I wan—"

"Here now, Kate," Turner said, getting abruptly to his feet while glancing from Jessie to Kate in confusion. "If Miss Forbes has other business, we mustn't detain her."

"Jessie, please," Kate murmured.

"Good day, then." Jessie didn't trust herself anywhere near Ken Turner another minute. If he put his hands on Kate again within her sight, she'd have to thrash him.

Before Kate could answer, Jessie tipped her hat once to Kate, whirled Star's head around, and spurred the horse sharply. Kate stepped away from Ken and stared after the rapidly retreating figure, her heart sinking. She had wanted so much to see her, and now she had hurt her. That was the last thing she had ever meant to do. She barely heard Ken as he informed her that he had news of some import to discuss. All she could hear was the receding thunder of hooves and the fading jingle of spurs.

Chapter Fifteen

That evening, sitting with Ken Turner and her parents in the parlor, Kate felt especially uneasy. Ken's polite but proprietary manner was becoming more difficult to tolerate every day, and his subtle but persistent caresses harder to avoid. The longer she spent trying to act as if nothing were wrong, the more certain she became that she needed to make a decision. She had to make clear to Ken and her parents that the union they all expected was not to be, but when she contemplated trying to explain her reasons for not being inclined to marry the man, even to herself, she faltered. It was more than that she did not love Ken Turner—for surely she did not—it was that she couldn't help but feel that there was something vital about her own heart she did not understand. When she could bear the social pleasantries and forced cheeriness no longer, she pleaded a headache and escaped to the quiet of her room.

There she lay staring into the darkness, struggling to understand her feelings. It had been agony not to see Jessie these past weeks. To finally see her that afternoon without being able to say how much she had missed her was even worse. The pain in Jessie's eyes haunted her. When she'd ridden away, Kate had feared that her own heart might break. She needed someone to talk to; she needed help. And she knew of only one place to go.

❖

Kate hesitated outside Mae's door, her confidence suddenly waning. When she awakened early that morning after a restless night, what she needed to do had seemed so clear to her. Now that she was here, she wasn't so certain anymore. Finally, she forced herself to knock.

"Kate!" Mae hastily tied her robe and gestured Kate into her room. The sun had barely risen, and since she kept late hours, she had only just been to bed. The sight of Kate at her door at such an hour brought only one thing to mind—Jessie. "What is it? Did something happen?"

"No...I just need...Can I talk with you, Mae?" Kate stood awkwardly just inside the threshold. She had never been in Mae's bedroom before, and the sudden intimacy of the moment embarrassed her. She looked away from the turned-down bedclothes and tried not to think about Mae's state of undress.

"Sure, honey. It must be important to get you here at this hour." Mae gestured to two chairs on either side of a small dressing table. "Sit down."

Kate sat quickly, afraid that she might suddenly lose her resolve and run. Mae's sharp eyes took in the tremor in Kate's hands and the uneasiness in her expression. She pulled a chair close.

"What *is* it, Kate?" she asked softly.

Tears brimmed behind Kate's lashes. "Mae, Ken Turner intends to speak to my father about marriage."

Mae was not particularly surprised. There wasn't much going on around town that she didn't eventually hear about. She had hoped that the rumors about Turner and Kate were true and that there was a match in the making. But looking at Kate now, she began to doubt it. "You don't look too happy about it. Isn't that what a girl like you would want? I should think he'd make a good catch, well respected and responsible and all that."

Bitterly Kate said, "Oh, you're quite right. He *is* a fine man, and I have nothing against him. But..." She struggled for the words.

"But what, honey?"

"I don't love him!"

Mae laughed, although there was an edge to it. "Do you think you'll be the first woman to make a match with a man she doesn't love?"

"But I don't want to spend my life with someone I don't love."

"Love doesn't put a roof over your head, Kate, or feed you, or earn you respect from your neighbors. I know." Mae eyed her sharply. "Listen. If he provides for you and doesn't mistreat you or disgrace you, you may find after a while that you love him. The heart does funny things, sometimes. And if not, you'll be no different than a lot of other women and better off than many."

Kate was shocked. She could well believe that not everyone enjoyed the kind of love that inspired poetry. But what Mae was suggesting seemed so cold and calculated. "I won't marry him just for that," she said with finality.

"Then wait for a fella more to your choosing," Mae acquiesced, having heard that stubborn tone in Kate's voice before. "You're young yet."

Kate hesitated, trying to find a way to express the question that kept raising itself in her mind. "What if—what if there's someone else?"

Mae had been expecting something like this, but the girl's honesty surprised her. "Is there someone else?"

"Yes." Now that she'd said it, she felt a rush of relief.

"Who is it?" Mae needed to hear the words. Maybe she was wrong. Because if she wasn't, she didn't know quite what she would say.

"It's Jessie," Kate answered, filled with sudden wonder. "I love Jessie." After so many weeks of not seeing, of being so close but not knowing, saying the words made everything clear. Now she understood why she felt so lonely and lost whenever they parted, and why she lay awake at night searching for ways to see her again. *It's Jessie who makes me feel special and cared for. It's Jessie who makes my spirit soar and my heart lift with happiness. It's Jessie I love.*

"I've been wondering if you'd ever figure that out," Mae said quietly.

Kate drew a surprised breath. "You knew?"

Mae laughed darkly. "I was pretty sure. But I was hoping you wouldn't keep on, that you'd marry your Mr. Turner and settle down the way you should."

"But why?" Kate asked, hearing Mae's opposition but still not comprehending it. *How can it be bad when what I feel for Jessie seems so right?*

"Why? Because of Jessie, for Lord's sake!" Kate's obvious naïveté finally ignited Mae's anger. Seething, she got to her feet. "You *say* that you love her. She'll love you, too, you know. Probably already does. Do you have any idea what that's going to do to her?"

Kate was stunned by the vehemence in her voice. "I don't understand."

"Jessie's been waiting her whole life for this, and she doesn't even know it," Mae continued as if she hadn't heard. "You'll let her believe, Kate, and then you'll leave her."

"No," Kate said. "I won't. I love her."

"Be reasonable, Kate! Your parents will never allow it, your friends will turn away, and if you try to hide it, the lies will wear you down. Sooner or later you'll leave her because loving her will be too hard. That will destroy her."

"No!" Kate repeated passionately. "I won't hurt her. I couldn't hurt her. Believe me, Mae, I won't change."

Mae sighed in frustration, uncertain whether to go on. But Kate had come to her, and there might not be another time. "You're young. When you're young, blood runs high. I *believe* you've got feelings for her. I do." She took a breath. "But *think* what you're saying. If you let Jessie love you, how long do you think it will be before Jessie wants to love you like…like a man loves a woman?"

Kate felt her face redden, but she would not avert her gaze. She thought about the way her heart raced when Jessie was near, the way her breath tripped when she looked into Jessie's eyes, and the way she trembled at the barest touch of Jessie's hand. She envisioned Jessie, sweat-dampened and dusty and so incredibly beautiful, and she was suddenly warm all over. She *knew* what she felt. She studied Mae calmly. "And you, Mae. Could you love her like that?"

"I would now, if she'd let me." Mae's expression was proud, but her eyes were sad.

"Does she know?" Kate asked gently.

Mae's smile was wan. "She's an innocent about such things."

"I didn't realize." Kate felt an odd sympathy for the other woman, although she supposed she should feel jealous. "I wouldn't have come—"

"Ah, honey," Mae said, "it wouldn't matter none. I saw the way things were going the first time I saw the two of you walking together."

Kate blushed. "You could tell?"

Mae nodded. "And then Jess would be showing up in the saloon at all hours, out of sorts and not knowing why her heart was aching. You didn't need to tell me what I already knew."

"Do you think…do you really think she…feels for me?"

"Search your heart, honey, and you answer that."

Kate rose slowly, understanding so much more than she had just minutes before. She touched Mae's arm as she left. "Thank you."

Mae looked after her, admiring her grit but praying that she'd come to her senses before it was too late.

Jessie came around the side of the barn, stopped abruptly, and gaped at the buckboard pulled up in her yard. That wasn't what grabbed her by the throat, though, and punched the breath from her chest. It looked a lot like Kate standing on her front porch, a linen-covered straw basket at her feet. It had been only a day or two since she had seen her with that Turner fellow out on the range. She'd been in a foul temper ever since, and she hadn't wanted to think too long about what that meant. In fact, she had been working harder than ever just so she *wouldn't* have to think about it. But she still recalled his arm around Kate's waist, like he owned her, and just remembering it made her want to curse. She had been afraid that Kate might never visit again, and now, here she was.

Jessie broke into a run and took the stairs two at a time. She skidded to a halt inches from her visitor. "Kate?" She couldn't keep the note of elation from her voice.

"Hello, Jessie."

"What are you doing here?" Jessie looked around, perplexed. "Where's John Emory?"

"He isn't here. I came by myself." Kate wanted to laugh at the open amazement on Jessie's face, but she took note of the flicker of worry that lingered there as well and added quietly, "I needed to see you."

"Come inside," Jessie held the screen door for her. "It's too hot out here already, and it isn't even noon."

Kate lifted the basket she had packed and stepped into the cool, dark hallway. She waited for Jessie to lead the way, following her through to the library.

As soon as they were seated in the two stuffed chairs facing the empty fireplace, Jessie asked, "How did you ever get your parents to let you come?"

"They think I'm at the Schroeders', helping Hannah."

Jessie looked shocked. "Lord, Kate."

Finally, Kate laughed. She was so glad to see her. "They don't expect me home until tonight, and I just couldn't wait until John Emory had the time to bring me."

"What's so important?" Jessie asked, her blue eyes clouded with concern. "Are you all right?"

"Last night Ken Turner asked me to marry him," Kate said quietly.

"Oh." Jessie stood up quickly and paced to the fireplace, needing distance. Some hard deep pain was threatening to break loose inside her, and she wanted to run. She wanted to be alone, because she didn't think she'd be able to weather this news in Kate's presence. Willing her legs to stay in place, she closed her eyes for just a minute, trying to get her bearings. She was having a little trouble catching her breath. She swallowed around the lump in her throat, but her voice still came out choked. "I—That's grand, Kate," she managed.

Kate rose too and hurried to her side. When she rested her hand on Jessie's arm, she felt her trembling. The thought that she'd upset her brought tears to her eyes. "It's not what you think, Jessie. I told him no."

Jessie was desolate, her mind aswirl with confusion. All she could think was that Kate would be gone. "I don't understand," she whispered. "Why?"

"I told him no, Jessie," Kate murmured, very close to her now, "because it's you I love."

A strange pounding began in Jessie's chest. Kate's words suddenly set her world straight. All the restless yearnings that had plagued her these past weeks vanished like mist in the sunlight. She wanted to say and do a thousand things, but all she could manage was to look into

Kate's eyes. They were so dark, so warm, and so welcoming.

"Kate," she breathed, her voice low, "I...I don't know what to say. I—"

"Shh." Kate touched her fingers to Jessie's lips, silencing her gently. "I don't want you to say anything, Jessie darling." She laid her cheek against Jessie's shoulder and threaded her arms around Jessie's waist. "I just want you to hold me."

A soft sigh escaped Jessie's lips. She stood very still, aware of Kate against every inch of her. Kate's words, the press of her body so near, the sudden knowing of what she'd wanted for so long all made the blood rush hot through her veins. She put trembling hands on Kate's waist, marveling at her softness. Very slowly, afraid that Kate might step away, she brushed her face over Kate's thick hair, closing her eyes as the sweet fragrance engulfed her. Longing twisted through her, and she groaned faintly.

Kate listened to the beat of Jessie's heart as contentment warred with something much more urgent—a swift stab of pleasure that bordered on pain. "Oh," she murmured, leaning harder into Jessie and drawing her closer.

"What is it?" Jessie asked hoarsely, her throat tight. So many feelings assaulted her she couldn't think. Holding Kate in her arms, she felt a mixture of tenderness and wanting so fierce she ached. "Kate, what's wrong?"

At last, Kate lifted her gaze to Jessie's face and found her expression hot and wild. Kate forgot to breathe for a long moment as Jessie's eyes devoured her. "I don't know," she gasped at last. "I want—oh, Jessie... I—don't know what I want." As she spoke, she steadily stroked Jessie's back, her shoulders, her chest—needing to feel her, wanting to get closer to her. She wasn't aware of anything save a craving more critical than anything she had ever known. "I think about you," she murmured, pushing her fingers into Jessie's hair, pulling the taller woman's head closer to her own. "I think about you—touching me."

Jessie was sure she was about to die. Her heart hammered in her chest, her lungs burned, and her legs threatened to give out. She tightened her grasp on Kate's waist, pulling her hard against her front, wanting her near, aching to tell her how much she needed her. How much she loved her. She had no words, but her heart knew. She dipped her head, closing that final distance between them, and pressed her mouth gently to Kate's, letting the soft certainty of her kiss speak for her.

Kate's lips parted initially in surprise, then in wonder. Jessie's kiss, tender at first, grew firmer as Kate tightened her fingers in Jessie's hair and, as naturally as breathing, skimmed her tongue over Jessie's lips. Jessie groaned again and Kate swayed in her arms, heat humming through her limbs like a fever, making her muscles weak and her head light. What she felt in Jessie's embrace was more than pleasure, more than passion. It was an unbearable hunger that threatened to undo her. She drank the sweetness of Jessie's mouth, quenching a thirst older than time.

When she could bear to pull her mouth away from those sweet kisses, she managed to say, "Oh my. What you make me feel! Never—I never imagined."

Consumed with arousal, Jessie buried her face in Kate's neck, unable to speak. Her stomach churned with an agony of desire. She had no way to control what she had never expected, and she moaned helplessly with the ache of wanting her. She framed Kate's face with trembling hands, finding those sweet lips once again, barely mindful of the ferocity of her caresses. Finally, kisses were not enough. "I need you, I need you," she murmured helplessly.

"Yes. Oh, Jessie, yes," Kate cried, unable to say what she desperately craved, but trusting Jessie to show her.

"Come lie with me, Kate?" Jessie dared ask, knowing only that she needed to touch Kate or die.

Kate nodded wordlessly, secure in the tenderness of Jessie's gaze.

Taking Kate's hand, Jessie led her gently up the stairs to her bedroom. A large four-poster bed that had been her parents' occupied the center of the room on a broad, braided rug. They stood close together, hands clasped, just inside the door, hesitating on the threshold of surrender.

"I love you, Kate," Jessie whispered, her voice breaking. She shuddered, wanting Kate so much that she was afraid to move. She feared that once she touched her, she would lose the last of her control. "I...I don't want to hurt you."

Kate smiled, sensing every ripple of desire in Jessie's slender body and recognizing every flicker of longing in her face. Stepping away, she watched Jessie's expression as she slowly released the ties on her bodice and slipped the dress from her shoulders. She loosened her corset and unhooked it, her pulse racing as she heard Jessie's quick intake of breath. Covered only by a light chemise, she returned to Jessie's arms. Her nipples, taut under the thin material, brushed against the rough denim of Jessie's shirt, and she gasped in surprise at the jolt of excitement that coursed through her. Jessie's hands were on her again, on her skin now. And everywhere she touched, Kate burned.

"I want to see you," Kate beseeched, her fingers working at the buttons on Jessie's shirt.

Jessie stood motionless, a fine mist of sweat breaking out on her face. Kate's breasts strained the cotton slip, shadows of pink nipples firm and clearly visible. Jessie cupped Kate's breasts in her palms, and Kate swayed against her, moaning softly. Jessie stilled, afraid that if she moved, the great dam inside her would burst and she would do something to frighten Kate. She ached to touch her, everywhere. Everywhere. Always. Hesitantly, she rubbed her fingers over Kate's nipples.

Biting her lip, Kate struggled to see through a haze of arousal. She finally loosened all the buttons on Jessie's shirt and slid it off her shoulders. "Oh!" she cried when she saw the still-fresh scar on Jessie's chest. She pressed her lips to it, her hands tenderly stroking Jessie's breasts.

"Kate, oh Kate. I can't bear it." Jessie groaned deep in her throat, lost. When Kate's lips found her nipple in a soft kiss, she broke. She picked Kate up in her arms and carried her in a few quick strides to the bed and laid her on the worn cotton coverlet. Leaning over her, naked from the waist up, she braced her arms on either side of Kate's body. She kissed her again, on her mouth, on her neck, not gently this time, but with a primal ferocity that had simmered unheeded all her life. Every kiss stoked her need. She reached for Kate's chemise, the last barrier, and stopped herself. "Kate?" she implored desperately, shivering with the ache in her depths.

"Yes, yes." Kate fumbled with Jessie's heavy belt, arching beneath her touch. Her voice was unrecognizable to her own ears. "Hurry, Jessie, please. I want to feel you against me!"

Swiftly, Jessie kicked off her boots and stripped the pants from her thighs. Kate lifted her chemise over her head, removed the remaining obstacle between them, and waited, naked and unafraid.

"Oh, lord," Jessie groaned as her gaze swept over Kate's body, taking in her full, firm breasts and the dark triangle of hair at the base of her abdomen. She lay down upon her, carefully, guided by instinct. She found the places that made Kate sigh, first with her fingers and then, needing more, with her lips. She tasted her, drank her, devoured her, all the while thrilling to the soft sound of Kate's cries. When Kate arched from the bed, body taut and trembling, Jessie hesitated, afraid of her own desire.

"Jessie," Kate murmured, her eyes closed, her face flushed with arousal. She found Jessie's hand and drew those fingers to the heat between her legs, lifting her hips to allow Jessie inside. "Please."

Jessie almost whimpered as the hot slick folds surrounded her fingers, resting her forehead on Kate's breast as she slowly, carefully entered her. Kate thrust against Jessie's palm, seemingly unaware of the small incoherent sounds escaping her throat. Jessie's chest constricted, her head throbbed, and a terrible pressure pounded through her limbs. She bit her lip and tried to hold onto reason.

Kate's eyes flew open in surprise. She grasped Jessie's shoulders convulsively, and pushed hard, once, against Jessie's fingers. Then she was gone, shattering into a thousand separate moments of pleasure, trembling and crying Jessie's name.

As Kate clung to her, Jessie lost her fight for control. She brought her leg over Kate's, frantic for relief, and exploded at first contact. Her breath was wrenched from her on a long, deep cry as she collapsed, exhausted, into Kate's waiting arms.

Kate awakened to the warm sun on her skin. It seemed to be late afternoon, and the air in Jessie's room was still and heavy. She lay in silence, eyes closed, enjoying the weight of Jessie's hand on her breast. Her body felt languid and full from the effects of their loving, and she smiled to herself with the memory of their pleasure. She thought of Jessie touching her, so gentle and careful, and how she'd ached to feel her closer—in her heart, and in her body. She loved Jessie— wanted her—with every part of her, and, recalling the sonnets of Mr. Shakespeare, understood now the joy in those songs of love.

Eventually, she opened her eyes. Jessie lay facing her, looking terribly innocent and vulnerable as she slept. Struck with the need to touch her, Kate gently explored the line of her brow, the angle of her cheek, and the soft curve of her lips. She raised herself so that she could see all of her, marveling at her loveliness. Jessie's body was like her, strong but secretly so tender. She lightly traced her fingers over the smooth column of her neck and along the edge of each delicate collarbone. Bending her head, she felt the softness of Jessie's breasts with her lips. When Jessie stirred and moaned in her sleep, Kate smiled. She wanted to pleasure her as she had been pleasured. Loving was a gift, and she sought to give what she had been given.

Tenderly, she curled her fingers in the blond hair between her lover's legs and kissed first her abdomen and then the pale skin in the hollow of her thigh.

"I love you," she whispered between kisses. It was so simple and so true. How could she not have known? "From the first moment. Oh, Jessie. I love you."

She stroked the silk-soft flesh of Jessie's thighs, then higher, seeking the wet warmth she knew was there, teasing each delicate fold between her fingertips until Jessie moaned and shook.

"Kate," Jessie murmured hoarsely, "Kate, what are you doing?"

"Shh, lie still. I'm loving you." Kate pulled Jessie close, continuing the steady caresses between her thighs. Emboldened by the urgent motion of Jessie's hips, she pressed her thumb to the stiff, engorged prominence and circled it, knowing Jessie as she knew herself.

"Oh, I…that's…" Jessie turned her face to Kate and trembled. "Please…I…"

"So beautiful," Kate sighed, lost in the wonder of loving her.

About to shatter, Jessie clutched her, her words trailing off to desperate pleas.

Unconsciously, Kate followed Jessie's body, matching her motions to Jessie's strangled cries. When Jessie arched, tight and trembling, Kate strummed her fingers hard and brought her home.

Chapter Sixteen

Jessie pulled the buckboard up behind the Schroeder house as the sun, a flaming fireball, dropped low and began to disappear behind the distant hills. She turned on the rough wooden seat to look at the young woman beside her. Her heart swelled with awe, the way it did when she stood—feeling small—before the majesty of the endless land and sky that sustained her. She was humbled at being entrusted with Kate's heart, and still stunned at the immense wonder of making love with her.

"I don't want to let you go," Jessie said softly. Kate's hand had rested on her thigh the entire hour it had taken her to drive into town, and Jessie didn't want her to move it. Ever. She questioned the rightness of being with Kate no more than she questioned the rightness of rising each morning to work her land. The places in her heart that had lain empty and waiting were filled. Her life seemed whole and all of a piece with Kate by her side. For her, it was simply the truth of things, and she thought no further than that. Loving Kate was right. "I never want you anywhere but with me."

"I don't want to leave you, either." Kate's face was flushed with more than the August heat. She had never experienced such an awakening of self, so suddenly, in both body and mind. She had known, when barely in her teens, that she did not desire the future that was expected for her, but try as she might, she could not picture any other. Oh, she had heard of women who struck off on their own, many of them traveling into the western territories as teachers and seamstresses and laundresses. But she had not seen herself among them. Nothing had ever prepared her for Jessie, or for what they had shared. But of one thing she was certain; she belonged with her. "I need to say hello to Hannah so that my day won't be a lie, but I'll come back to the ranch as soon as I can get away again. My mother is starting to get used to me driving into town alone. She doesn't need to know I'm coming to you."

"Maybe you should wait a bit. I don't want to cause trouble for you with your folks." Jessie meant the words, but the thought of even a few days apart from Kate made her hurt all over.

"You could never do that," Kate said, rubbing her hand along Jessie's leg. She knew little of what physical intimacies men and women enjoyed, having heard only veiled references from her mother and wild speculation from her girlfriends, but she knew what Jessie stirred in her. She knew what she held in her heart for this woman, and when that love echoed in her body, she welcomed it. Jessie's tenderness and passion fulfilled her. Why it was so, she could not say, and did not need to. "You're who I've been waiting for."

"I'm already missing you," Jessie confessed.

"I'll come to you again as soon as I can," Kate repeated firmly, needing to reassure herself as well as Jessie.

"It will be a trial waiting." Jessie struggled to describe her need, her fist opening and closing in frustration at her lack of words. She wanted Kate in her arms again; she wanted to hear her cries of abandon as she touched her. She shuddered with the memory. Her eyes sought Kate's, searching and filled with desire. "It's like I'm hungry for you."

"Jessie," Kate breathed, the wanting starting again. She closed her fingers over Jessie's fist. "I don't know what it is, but I can't stop thinking about being with you. Like we were today."

Jessie spoke quietly, watching night approach as the sky flamed into purples, pinks, and deep oranges. "I don't have words for what happened, Kate. I don't know if there *are* words for it." She looked back to Kate, her body rippling with tension. "But I know that I love you. Life wouldn't mean much to me now without you. That won't ever change."

Kate smiled, her heart filling with the tenderness of Jessie's sweet, sure vows. "I love you, too."

They smiled into one another's eyes, believing that love was all that mattered.

Hannah rinsed out the dishtowel and hung it over the wooden rod inside her back door, watching the two women in the buckboard through her kitchen window. They were only talking, and she couldn't hear their words, but she didn't need to. She was watching their faces. Jessie had that solemn, serious expression on her face, the one Thaddeus had worn when he was working his way up to proposing, and Kate gazed at Jessie the way every young woman in love looks at her beau.

She wondered why she wasn't more surprised. She supposed it was because she had lived more than half her life on the frontier, and she had learned that city ways didn't count for much out here. There were women without husbands due to famine or fancy or fate, and they did what they had to do to get by. Some married for safety, forgoing love; some, when widowed, stepped up to fill their men's shoes, managing families and farms on their own; and some came west with no intention of being anybody's wife right from the start. Living close to the bone, with death a constant shadow, you learned fast to take what goodness life sent your way when you could, because sorrow was just over the horizon.

Looking at the two of them together, she couldn't see much harm to the caring. But she wondered what Martha might think if she was ever to be faced with it.

"Hannah," Kate said breathlessly as she came through the door, "I'm so sorry I'm so late. I met Jessie and—"

Hannah shushed her with a shake of her head. "That's fine, Kate. I like your company, and I'm always happy to see you, but you don't need to feel obliged to spend your time over here. I don't expect there's anything you'll need to know that you won't find out when the time comes."

Kate nodded, only half listening as she watched Jessie untie her horse from the back of the buckboard and prepare to leave. Every movement of her graceful hands reminded Kate of the way they had felt on her body, and she grew warm with the memory. Jessie swung into the saddle, turned to the house, her eyes searching for Kate, and then she was gone with one last smile.

Kate turned away from the window to find Hannah regarding her speculatively. Her face flamed because she was certain that Hannah could read every thought.

Pulling a tray of biscuits from the oven, Hannah slid the flat metal onto a cooling stone on the counter. "Jessie Forbes is a fine young woman," she remarked, her back to Kate. "Works hard and turns an honest profit."

"Yes," Kate said cautiously.

Hannah wiped her hands on her apron and turned to regard Kate steadily. "Next time you should invite her in for a drink before she has to ride all that dusty way back to her ranch."

Kate struggled for words and finally whispered, "Thank you, Hannah."

"You're a sight for sore eyes, Montana," Mae said as she stepped up to the bar beside Jessie. "Seems I only see you anymore when someone's plugged you full of holes."

Jessie grinned sheepishly. "Hello, Mae. I was hoping you'd be around."

Mae studied her quizzically. "The sun's just set, Jess. The varmints won't be out for a while, so I'm not busy. Why don't you come sit a spell and tell me what brings you into town in the middle of the week?"

"How about you let me buy you dinner?" Jessie countered, wanting company. She had resisted going home because she knew the house would rattle with loneliness, and she already ached for Kate.

"I believe I'll take you up on that." Mae slipped her arm through Jessie's. When they had moved into the dining room, she once again regarded her friend curiously. She didn't think she'd ever seen Jessie look moody before. "What're you fretting about, Montana?"

"Hmm? Oh. Why, nothing," Jessie said quickly, blushing. She'd been thinking about waking up and feeling Kate's hands on her thighs, and about the way Kate knew just how to touch her in those spots that set her head to spinning, and how just when she didn't think she could stand another second without some part of her bursting, Kate had done just the right thing, and she *had* exploded. Remembering it brought the feelings back so strongly she gasped.

Mae leaned back in her chair, watching a flood of emotions play across Jessie's expressive features. *How she ever manages to win at poker, I don't know, because her face is an open book.* And what was written there made her heart sink. Jessie's eyes were a little hazy, and her skin was flushed under her tan. Her body almost quivered. Mae thought she could feel the heat radiating from her. Jessie Forbes looked like a woman who had been well loved, and recently.

She knew better than to ask, because Jessie was too honorable to tell. Instead, she casually asked, "What brings you in here today?"

"I drove Kate Beecher over to the Schroeder place," Jessie replied. She wanted to tell Mae about the extraordinary thing that had happened to her, but she barely had words for it herself. Plus, it was so intensely personal, so special, that she couldn't imagine sharing the details with anyone. "She was out my way, and it was getting late…so I brought her into town."

"Visiting, was she?"

"Yes." Jessie smiled, nodding absently as she recalled Kate whispering *I love you.*

"Way out there?"

"She wanted to see the ranch."

"How nice," Mae remarked coolly. "I hear tell that she and Ken Turner are courting."

Jessie shrugged. "I think that's mostly wishful thinking on his part."

Mae recognized the unwitting satisfaction in Jessie's voice. She didn't appear to be worried about Ken Turner. Not at all. *Oh Kate. What have you done?* She hoped that Kate knew what she was playing at, because she was willing to bet that Jessie didn't. From the looks of her, she was too far gone already to see trouble coming. "She *is* of marrying age, and I'm sure her folks are anxious to see her settled."

"I expect that Kate knows what she's about," Jessie said with certainty. "And I don't see as Ken Turner's who she wants."

As if what she wants matters! Do they think the Beechers will give their blessing to the two of them? Lord, what are they thinking? Mae lay her hand on Jessie's arm. "You know you've always got a friend here if you ever need one."

Jessie looked at her quizzically, then took Mae's fingers lightly in hers. "I'll remember, Mae."

Kate, her hair whipping behind her in the breeze, turned the buckboard expertly through the gates of the Rising Star ranch and looked expectantly toward the house. Her skin tingled with the familiar excitement that accompanied each visit. The sun had never felt so good, nor the air so clear. She pulled into the yard just as Jessie came out onto the porch. Kate drew a breath, seeing her again as if for the first time, only now her body held the memory of Jessie's caresses, and that alone was enough to stir her senses. She stepped onto the running board, her eyes dancing with happiness and the first awakening of desire as Jessie crossed the ground between them in quick, eager strides.

"Kate!" Jessie swung her exuberantly down from the wagon.

Kate laughed aloud and wrapped her arms around Jessie's neck, searching for Jessie's mouth with hers as her feet touched the ground. They stood together under the bright morning sky, lost in their embrace, as carefree as they would ever be.

After a moment, Jessie pulled her head back but kept her arms around Kate's waist. Flushed and breathless, she teased, "I thought you wanted shooting lessons?"

"I did," Kate murmured, amazed at the way Jessie's touch aroused her. Even hours after she returned home, she still tingled where Jessie's hands and lips had stroked her. She had never imagined love would feel like this. That love would be a thing of the mind and the heart, yes. But the *wanting!* That was something so unexpected she could think of little else. "Until just a moment ago."

"What changed your mind?"

Kate knew from the way Jessie's hands strayed over her back and the hoarse tone of her voice that her mind was not on the plans they had made either. Kate pressed her lips warmly against the tanned triangle of skin bared by Jessie's shirt. Playfully she said, "I really can't imagine."

Jessie, her eyes languid and full of promise, tilted Kate's chin up and grinned. "Maybe I can help you there."

"You mustn't tease me," she said, but her tone was unconvincing. Even more telling was the rapid rise and fall of her chest as her breath grew short. "We'd better go now, or I won't let you away for hours."

Jessie didn't let her go, but instead moved her lips close to Kate's ear. "We can always go later. And I don't think I can ride now." She kissed the sweet skin of Kate's neck, and they both groaned. "I'm about to forget myself altogether."

Kate pushed her away, but her fingers brushed lightly over Jessie's breasts. "Inside the house," she whispered, watching Jessie's color rise and her pupils grow large. "Quickly."

They made it to the bottom of the staircase before Jessie grabbed Kate and pressed her to the wall, fingers searching for the ties on her dress. Her hands were inside Kate's bodice an instant later, lifting her breasts free of their restraints.

"Lord, Kate," she groaned as she lowered her lips to Kate's hardening nipples, "I've missed you so."

Kate struggled to stand as a flood of arousal threatened to take her legs from under her. Her head fell back against the wall, and she curled her fingers in blond hair, pressing Jessie's face to her breasts. Jessie's tongue was on her, kindling a fire that spread downward with unchecked abandon. It was always like this, and never the same. Jessie's desire inflamed her, and every ounce of her flesh responded. She quickened in a heartbeat and teetered on the brink of dissolving for long agonizing, wonderful moments, crying Jessie's name, begging for her touch.

Sensing Kate's passion rising, Jessie became more insistent with her caresses. Kate trembled against her, and there was a desperate edge in her voice. With effort, she raised her lips from the sweet warmth of Kate's breast, gasping, "Wait. Let me take you to bed."

Kate managed to open her eyes and shook her head, her hands twisting in Jessie's shirt. Her eyes were huge, dark pools of yearning. "No," she choked. "No. Now. Now, please."

"Help me," Jessie demanded urgently, fired by Kate's need. She lifted the light cotton dress for Kate to hold and knelt before her. Gently, she pulled the final barriers aside and leaned forward, kissing the very center of Kate's desire. In response, Kate jerked against her and cried her name.

Jessie closed her eyes, her arms around Kate's hips, supporting her. She listened to her love while caressing her, tracing the soft swell of engorged tissues with her tongue, sucking gently as Kate sobbed with pleasure. She followed the rhythm and call of Kate's need, losing herself for long moments in the scent and taste of her. Kate's hands fluttered over her face and through her hair, leading her to the precious places she worshipped. She felt Kate grow and harden under her tongue and knew without telling that her release was near. She continued to stroke as Kate arched against her mouth, feeling her own heart stop as the pulse under her lips beat wildly.

She caught Kate as she was about to fall, standing quickly and gathering her into her arms. Still inflamed by the same consuming heat that had taken Kate, she kissed her fiercely. Her breath tore from her chest as she desperately pressed her hips forward.

"Kate," she groaned, barely able to see. "I—I need…" Her voice trailed off into a strangled sob as she buried her face against Kate's shoulder, shuddering.

"I know," Kate crooned, lightly caressing Jessie's fevered face. "I know." She slipped her hand between them, squeezing her palm to the soft material between Jessie's legs, cupping her. She smiled as Jessie moaned. Quickly, she pulled each button free, working her fingers under the material to find the desire waiting for her. As Kate squeezed the firm length of her, Jessie swayed, weak with the pleasure of it. Kate met each thrust of her hips with an answering tug until Jessie stiffened and groaned her release. When Jessie trembled in her arms, helpless and spent, Kate covered her damp face with kisses, glorying in the power of loving her.

Jessie carried their picnic basket to the buckboard with Kate close to her side, an arm linked in hers. Her body still tingled with the excitement they had just shared, and she couldn't stop grinning as she helped Kate up onto the seat.

"What?" Kate asked fondly, noting her satisfied expression.

"Just happy," Jessie answered, swinging up beside her. "Trying to figure out what I ever did to deserve you."

Kate moved her hand to Jessie's thigh, leaning against her as Jessie started the horses out of the yard. "You're just you, and you don't ever have to do anything except love me."

Jessie glanced at her, suddenly serious. "I will, Kate. Always."

"Mmm. Show me your land, darling." Kate snuggled closer, still languorous and content from their loving.

Jessie drove slowly through the lowlands and hills, stopping frequently to point things out and answer Kate's questions. Their route took in the summer grazing lands, sprinkled with wandering herds of horses, and the out cabins where she and the men stayed during branding times and roundups. From a hilltop overlooking impossibly green meadows, Jessie indicated the steeply rising mountains that bordered her land to the west.

"Those peaks are a natural protection for the highland meadows where the horses winter. When it starts to frost in the fall, we round up all the young and any pregnant mares and bring them down to that small canyon I showed you earlier. If the winter is really bad, they can't forage, and we feed them."

"Oh, Jessie," Kate exclaimed, awed by the scope of it all. "It's so beautiful. You must love it very much."

"I never thought I could love anything more." Jessie took Kate's hand and brought it to her lips. "Until you."

Slipping her arm around Jessie's waist, Kate rested her head on Jessie's shoulder, stroking her arm through the soft cotton of her shirt. She thought how much she loved her simple strength and gentle heart. "Jessie," she murmured softly.

Jessie kissed her temple. "What?"

"I don't want things to ever change." Jessie was quiet so long that Kate leaned away to look at her face. "What's wrong?"

"I can't stand being apart from you so much," Jessie admitted at last, her voice low and tight. "I want us to lie down together at night and sleep side by side. I want to wake up with you." She looked at Kate, her eyes troubled. "I want—well—if I was a man, I'd want to marry you."

Kate's heart turned over. "Oh, Jessie," she breathed. "I love you."

Jessie searched Kate's face, finding all the courage she needed in that tender gaze. "I want you to come live with me, Kate. Will you?"

It was Kate's turn to be silent. When she spoke, her tone was anguished. "I want to. I want to be with you, married or not, for all my life." She stroked Jessie's cheek, her throat so tight she could barely speak. "But I don't know how."

"If you want to, that's all that matters to me right now. We'll figure it out," Jessie said, cradling Kate's hand and kissing her palm. "We've got time."

She climbed down and reached up for Kate. "Now, how about we give you that shooting lesson."

Kate tried not to think of anything else as Jessie stood behind her, occasionally wrapping her arms around her to steady the Winchester, whispering encouragement in her ear. She even managed to hit the targets Jessie picked out now and then, but she couldn't quite rid herself of thoughts about confronting her parents. *How will I explain my desire to be with Jessie? How can I make them see that this is truly what I want for my life? And what will I do if they refuse?*

Chapter Seventeen

S ummer passed quickly, and the fall days were upon them before they knew it. Jessie's joy at returning home after hours on the range to unexpectedly find Kate quietly reading on the porch or preparing a meal in the kitchen was undiminished by the passage of time. Their love was simple and pure, and they grew closer as surely and naturally as two branches on the same tree, drawing nourishment from the same spring. The moments they spent together, talking and loving, were precious, bringing Jessie more happiness than she had dared dream of only a few months before. Still, she found herself wanting more.

Days—sometimes even a week or more—passed between Kate's visits, and during those times, she suffered from more than loneliness. She couldn't help but think of Ken Turner, who she knew still paid court to Kate. It tormented her to think that he might touch Kate, when *she* could not even arrive unannounced at her door, asking only for the pleasure of sitting by her side.

Each time she walked Kate to the buckboard and watched her drive away, it was harder to let her go. The nights when she lay down alone were colder and longer than any she could ever recall. She was lonely in a way she never had been before, because now there were places in her heart that only Kate could fill.

"Kate?" Jessie asked late one afternoon, lying naked with Kate in her arms under a heavy quilt. A fire burned in the hearth in the bedroom. Kate's back was to her front, and she buried her face in Kate's thick hair, smoothing her hands slowly over Kate's stomach until she cupped her breasts in her hands.

Kate stilled Jessie's movement, pressing her palms over Jessie's hands. "I can't think when you do that," Kate admonished lightly, but there was no disapproval in her tone. She loved Jessie's hands on her. "What is it?"

Closing her eyes, Jessie sighed, trying to shut out every sensation but Kate. She couldn't, as much as she wished to. "Winter comes early out here, Kate. It will snow soon."

"Yes." Kate's grip on Jessie's hands tightened.

"It's not safe for you to come here any longer," Jessie continued, each word feeling like it was tearing a piece of her heart away as she spoke it. "You could be caught in a blizzard and freeze to death quicker than a minute."

"What are you saying?"

"You can't come out here alone, and before long, not even with John Emory."

"I can't stay away," Kate whispered. "I can't be without you." She couldn't imagine a week, let alone the long months of winter, separated from her.

"I can't have anything happening to you." Jessie pulled her even closer. "I'm not made strong enough for that. Promise me you won't drive out here alone again."

"If I come with John, we can't lie together."

"I know," Jessie said, her misery apparent in her voice, "but we'll see each other."

"It's not enough. I need you like this." Kate pressed Jessie's hands to her breasts. "I need you."

"Lord, Kate," Jessie groaned, her mouth hot against Kate's neck. "I need you, too—like water and air. But I can't have you in danger. I won't be able to breathe for the worrying."

Kate knew Jessie was right, and she would never worry her, even though it would be devastating to go all winter without seeing her. She turned within the circle of her arms, searching her face, seeing the melancholy in her eyes. "We must find another way." She sought Jessie's mouth, kissing her lightly at first, then with urgent hunger. She drew away with a small cry. "I *won't* be without you."

"I'll come into town when I can," Jessie gasped. "Maybe you could come to the hotel?"

Even as she said it, she knew that it was impossible. The weather was unpredictable at best in the foothills of the Rockies, and even if she could leave the ranch, how would she get a message to Kate to let her know that she had come? And meeting at the hotel? Impossible. There was no way that they could ever keep *that* fact from Kate's parents for long. Plus, part of her resisted the idea of meeting Kate for an afternoon's passion, as if that was all there was between them. She never tired of loving her for hours on end—she ached for Kate in her arms—but she took just as much joy in raising her eyes from some bit of work to find Kate sitting nearby with a book in her hands.

"I must speak to my parents," Kate said, knowing the time had come at last. She could not go on indefinitely avoiding Ken Turner's persistent demands, nor could she pretend to her parents that her reluctance was only because she was not certain that she wished to be *his* wife. Having lain with Jessie, she could never be any man's wife. Jessie was her heart. "I'll make them understand."

"I'll come with you," Jessie said firmly, moving to get up. "They'll never need worry for your safety nor your care, not as long as I live, nor after either. I owe them the comfort of knowing that."

"Wait," Kate cried, holding her fast. "We have time before I need to be back." She stretched out in Jessie's arms, her legs entwining naturally with those of her taller lover. "I'll not let go of you yet."

Jessie smiled, turning so Kate lay beneath her, and lowered herself gently upon her. Her chest filled with an almost unbearable sensation of tenderness and wonder, and she set about showing Kate just how much she cherished her. With her lips, with her mouth, with her work-roughened hands turned to velvet on Kate's sweet skin, she told her. Her kisses carried the promises, and her touch conveyed the certainty that she so often had no words to express. *I will love you*, Jessie's caresses vowed, *with all my being, for all my life. You are my reason and my answer and my purpose*, her fingers pledged, each knowing stroke carrying Kate closer to fulfillment.

"I love you, Kate, I love you," she whispered, her face pressed to Kate's neck. An inarticulate moan escaped Kate's throat as she arched under Jessie's hands.

Jessie held her until she quieted and caressed her lightly while she dozed. She could no longer remember what her existence had been like before Kate, and she could not imagine a life without her now.

❖

"I want to come with you," Jessie said again, stubbornly insistent.

They sat in the buckboard not far from Kate's house; Star was tied to the back, waiting patiently. Darkness was falling, and the night was cold. Kate was wrapped in a heavy wool blanket, her cloak fastened tightly around her. Jessie wore a heavy sheepskin coat with her hat pulled low. Her hands were bare. Their breath hung in small white clouds, a reminder that they had very little time before nature made separation inevitable.

"I know you do. But let me talk with them first." Kate slipped her fingers from her glove and took Jessie's hand. It was warm. Her head ached just thinking about what her mother was going to say. "They might need just a while to get used to the idea."

"They need to know what I feel for you," Jessie persisted. It was only proper that she speak up. "I don't want you to do this alone, Kate. It's not right."

Kate looked at her quickly, hearing a note of worry in her tone. "What are you thinking?"

"I just want to stand by your side."

"You don't think that I'll let them talk me out of it, do you?"

"No, never," Jessie said firmly. "I know what you feel—I know it when you touch me and when you ask for my touch. I don't suppose there's a word for what we are to each other, but I know that you are the only one I'll ever love. I want us to be together, and the closest word I know to that is *married*."

"Yes, I want that, too." Kate set her shoulders with resolve. "You go have dinner at the hotel and then come back to the house around eight o'clock. We can all talk then."

"Oh, Kate! I can't eat!" Jessie protested. "My stomach feels like a nest of rattlers."

Kate felt dizzy with apprehension, too. "Then go to the bar and talk to Frank."

Jessie didn't like it, but they were Kate's parents, and she supposed it made some sense to get them used to the idea before she showed up on their doorstep. She bit back a further protest as she helped Kate down from the wagon. Kate swayed suddenly, and Jessie caught hold of her.

"What's wrong?" she asked, alarmed at Kate's pallor.

Kate smiled tremulously, oddly breathless. She shook her head. "It's nothing. I'm just nervous." She reached a hand to brush Jessie's cheek. "I'm fine. You go on now. I'll see you in a little while."

Watching Kate walk away from her, Jessie stood by the side of the buckboard, a sinking feeling in her chest. She felt helpless and, unexpectedly, very much afraid.

"Something wrong with Frank's whiskey?" Mae asked. "You been standing there with that same drink in front of you for better than an hour."

"No," Jessie said, her voice hollow. "His whiskey's fine." She tossed it back swiftly and tapped the empty glass on the bar for another.

"What's gotten into you?" Mae was taken aback by the bleak tone of her voice. "You look like a whipped dog."

"I feel like one. Probably worse."

Mae motioned to Frank for a bottle. "Bring your glass, and let's sit for a minute. You'd best tell me what's going on."

Jessie followed her to a table in the far corner of the saloon and downed another shot of whiskey she couldn't taste. She reached for the bottle, but Mae stopped her.

"Talk, Jess."

With her empty glass cupped between her fingers and her voice rough with pain, Jessie spoke of Kate, and their love, and their plans. When she reached the part where she had gone back to the Beecher house that evening, she finally raised her eyes and met Mae's.

"Her father came to the door and stepped out onto the porch when he saw that it was me," Jessie said unsteadily. "He was polite. He told me Kate was indisposed and could not see me. And he said it's best that I not come around again, seeing that Kate would be very busy soon preparing for her wedding to Mr. Turner."

She grasped the bottle, and this time, Mae made no move to stop her. Her hand shook as she filled her glass. "He never even raised his voice, but the look on his face could have frozen a pond in the middle of summer." She emptied the glass and set it down hard. "I'd rather he'd've hit me."

Mae tried to absorb the tale. As she'd listened, her emotions had run the gamut from despair to faint hope. Her initial reaction had been shock. She hadn't known what to expect after Kate's visit, but it hadn't been this. Hearing Jessie tell it, watching her face, Mae could see how much she loved the girl, and it almost broke her heart. Then, when she heard that Kate's father had put a stop to the relationship, her response had been relief and, God help her, happiness.

"Maybe it's for the best, Jess," she said gently. *You'll get over her. She's not right for you.* She wanted to say it, but part of her didn't believe it. She remembered the blaze in Kate's eyes when she had said that she loved Jessie, and she heard the torment in Jessie's voice now. *Lord, they love each other right enough.*

"How?" Jessie's eyes were wounded as she met Mae's gaze. "How could it be for the best? I love her, and she loves me."

"Her parents will never accept it," Mae said softly. "A girl like her is supposed to be married. They won't know no other way."

"What about what *she* wants? What about Kate's happiness?"

Mae couldn't help but laugh, but there was no humor in her voice. "Lord's sake, Jess. Whenever did the feelings of a woman matter in these things?"

"Kate matters, Mae," Jessie said firmly, a spark of life returning to her eyes. "She matters to me more than anything in this world."

"More than the ranch?" Mae wanted Jessie to see the hopelessness of this wild dream. "Because if you think they're just gonna let her move on out there with you, without a fight, you're more drunk than a few whiskeys would make you."

Jessie was quiet a long time, thinking about the look on Martin Beecher's face. She knew when a man could not be swayed. "No, I don't suppose they'll *let* her come."

"Don't do anything foolish, Montana," Mae said as tenderly as she could. She saw a cowboy approaching from the corner of her eye and, knowing he'd just get ugly if she tried to turn him away, rose with a quiet curse. "Some things aren't meant to be, even if they do seem right."

Jessie watched Mae walk away with the cowboy, sad to see her go. She sat for a long time, turning the empty glass on the scarred tabletop, until she knew what she must do. The only thing she could do, because her and Kate being together was the only thing that *was* right.

CHAPTER EIGHTEEN

K ate approached the Schroeders' back door the next morning burdened in body and soul. An overwhelming sense of hopelessness left her dazed. She had barely slept, her head ached horribly, and she hadn't been able to manage more than a bit of juice at breakfast. Though she had no idea how she would get through a morning with Hannah without crying, the thought of staying at home to face her mother's silent admonitions was even more daunting. As she slowly climbed the stairs to the porch, she was surprised to see Hannah Schroeder emerging in a rush, her expression expectant, as if she had been waiting for her to arrive.

"Come inside, Kate," she said kindly, holding the door for her. "It's freezing out here."

Kate nodded absently, but she was having trouble putting one foot in front of the other. Everything seemed so impossible. Faced with the harsh reality of her utter powerlessness to go against her parents' wishes, she felt like a prisoner in her own life. *I am a prisoner—of convention and custom and the narrow-minded views of the very people who say they love me. They wouldn't even listen to me—how can that be love?*

"Come stand by the stove. You're shaking," Hannah directed, guiding her into the kitchen.

"Thank you." Kate's throat was dry, almost parched. The heat from the ovens accosted her, and, for an instant, she felt dizzy. She swayed slightly, and Hannah slipped a protective arm around her waist to steady her. Kate loosened her scarf with trembling hands and slipped out of her cloak.

With a worried frown, Hannah passed a cool hand over Kate's forehead. "You look peaked. You'd best take care. Sally down at the dry goods store says there's quite a few people down with the grippe."

"I'm fine." Kate gave a tremulous smile, but her eyes brimmed with tears. *My heart is breaking. What do I care of the grippe?*

"Well," Hannah said quietly, "you've got a visitor. Go on in the parlor there. I'll bring you some biscuits and tea. You look like you could use something."

Confused, Kate didn't move. "A visitor?"

"Go on, now," Hannah urged gently.

Kate made her way through the quiet house toward the room at the end of the hall where she had met the Schroeders on her very first morning in New Hope. Looking back, she saw a stranger—barely more than a child—bright and eager and filled with expectations. She was a woman now, and all she could imagine was a dark future that held no hope of liberty or love. She stepped into the room and stumbled to a halt, stunned to see the familiar figure waiting by the window. She closed her eyes briefly, sure that she was dreaming.

"Jessie?" she whispered when she could speak.

"Kate."

And then she was running forward, and Jessie's arms were around her, and she was clinging to her, sobbing with a combination of joy and piercing sorrow. *Will this be the last time I hold you? Oh, my love...* She pressed her cheek to Jessie's shoulder, silently seeking shelter in her lover's embrace.

"My Kate," Jessie murmured into her hair, stroking her tenderly. "It's all right. It's all right."

But Kate knew that it would never be all right again. "Oh, Jessie. I was afraid when my father wouldn't let me speak to you last night that I might never see you again. But you didn't leave me."

"No, never," Jessie assured her swiftly, her heart thudding painfully at the thought. Feigning a confidence she didn't feel, she went on as steadily as she could. "What did they say to you? Tell me what happened, love."

Her mind still numb, Kate said, "My parents think I've become unbalanced. That the move out here from Boston has done things to me." She laughed harshly, a sob forming at the end. "Mother is sure that I've had some kind of breakdown, and Father thinks that being uprooted from home has caused me to suffer a lapse in judgment."

"Because you love me?"

Kate smiled through her tears. Jessie's steadfast presence settled her nerves, and she felt sanity returning after the nightmare of the previous evening. *This...this woman...this love, is real.*

When she spoke again, her voice was calmer. "No, my darling. Because I *don't* love Ken Turner. Or more to the point, because I won't marry him." At Jessie's look of confusion, she went on, "My mother actually tried to be somewhat understanding. She allowed that women often form 'close affections,' particularly during stressful times, but every woman knows that those friendships must take a second seat to the responsibilities of a wife. She says I simply need to see that."

Trying to make sense of a concept foreign to her, Jessie grew still. "They think that if you marry him you won't love me any more?"

"No," Kate said quietly. "As long as I don't see you and perform my wifely duties as expected with Ken, I don't think it matters to them at all if I love you or not. We will just not speak of it." She recalled the dark look in her father's eyes as he had pronounced that she would accept Ken Turner's proposal, which she should have done months ago, and that they would hear no more of her foolish desire to live at the Rising Star ranch with Jessie Forbes.

"Can they force you to marry him?"

"No, but if I refuse, there will be consequences."

"What does that mean?" Jessie clenched her jaw, fury and fear warring within. "They won't put you out, will they?"

"No, they love me, despite how it looks. They won't disown me."

"Well, that's something." Jessie sighed, grasping at any small glimmer of hope. "Maybe if we give them a little time and then talk to them again—together—we can make them understand."

Kate gazed into Jessie's face. She traced the strong line of Jessie's jaw with trembling fingers, aching with love for her and knowing how much she was about to hurt her. "My father was quite clear as to his intentions if I don't do as they say. If I fail to marry by the time the roads are passable in the Spring, they'll send me back to Boston. There's no way I can imagine of changing their minds. I'm so sorry, Jessie. I'm so sorry."

Her heart nearly broke as she watched the color drain slowly from Jessie's face and her expression collapse with pain. Watching tears form in her lover's eyes was worse than any agony she could suffer herself.

"Oh, Lord," Jessie whispered, terror making her shake. "They can't send you away." She gripped Kate's shoulders in a tortured grasp, her eyes wild. "Can they, Kate?"

"I *am* of age, but how can I defy them? I have neither funds of my own nor any real means of supporting myself. And where could I go?"

Jessie's temper flared, although her anger was not at Kate. "You can come to me. I *love* you, Kate. You belong with me!" She made an effort to control herself. "That's what you want, isn't it? That would make you happy?"

"Oh, Jessie. Of course!" Kate kissed her quickly. "You make me happier than I've ever been. You're the only thing that matters to me. You must know I love you with all my heart."

"Then come be with me," Jessie implored. Her voice broke, her throat tightening with love and fear and hope. "Please."

Kate stroked Jessie's arm tenderly. "Oh my love, if only I could. But my father would never allow it. He would know that I had gone to you, and he would come for me. I'm not sure what he would do, but I won't have you hurt by this."

"Hurt?" Jessie cried. "Hurt! What will I do if they take you from me? How do you think I could live after losing you? I'd have nothing without you."

Kate held Jessie tightly, as if that fragile bond alone could keep them together. "Nor I, without you."

Moments passed as they embraced, soothing and reassuring each other with murmurs of devotion and desperate kisses. Kate pressed her face to Jessie's neck. "I can't lose you. I love you so."

Jessie's voice was quiet and resigned. "Then we have to leave here. We'll go away, farther west to the Oregon territory. There's gold there still." She drew another deep breath, her resolve growing. "I can even pass for a man if there's need. It's happened before without my meaning it."

Kate drew a sharp breath. "No! You can't leave the ranch. It's your home!"

"There would be no home for me anywhere without you, Kate. I will not let you go."

Kate saw the certainty in Jessie's blue eyes, and something she needed to see even more—the love. "Oh, Jessie, I'm so sorry about your ranch."

"It's all right, love. Who knows, maybe we'll be able to come back after a season or two." Jessie smiled. Leaving the Rising Star would be like losing an arm or a leg, but life without Kate would be no life at all. There was no choice as to what needed to be done. "We'll need to leave very soon, before the mountain passes are snowed in."

Kate stepped away and drew a deep breath, feeling suddenly stronger. "When?"

"Before the end of the week."

"Yes," she answered, knowing this was right. An instant later she smiled, a firm resolute smile, realizing that for the first time in her life she *did* have a choice, and her choice was Jessie.

"When can you be ready to leave?" Jessie asked.

"Soon," Kate said purposefully. "There are only a few things that I want to bring, but I must gather them without my parents' notice. The day after tomorrow?"

Jessie nodded, already planning what she needed to buy on her way out of town. Most of what they would need for the trek she had at the ranch. She'd settle at the bank and talk to Jed. She could trust him. "We'll leave in two days, then."

"Oh my love, I'm so sorry that it's come to this."

Jessie held Kate firmly to her breast. "Don't be, Kate. Your love is all that matters to me."

❖

"I need to go home, Hannah." Kate looked out the kitchen window as Jessie rode out of the yard, feeling hopeful for the first time since the horrible scene with her parents. "I'm sorry I can't stay."

"No need to worry," Hannah said, packing some hot biscuits into a basket along with a jar of jam. "Take these. You'll be hungry sooner or later."

Kate smiled fondly. "You've been very kind. I don't know how my mother or I would have managed without all your help. Thank you."

Hannah looked at Kate steadily, noting the tear stains still damp on her cheeks and the hint of misery in her eyes. It wasn't any of her affair, but it was plain to see that the child was suffering. Seemed to her that Jessie Forbes had looked the same when she had come to the back door just after sunup, asking if she might wait for Kate. Didn't take much sense to see that something bad had happened, and she had a feeling she knew what it was. If it was Martin and Martha coming between those two, she didn't see any hope for the young ones. She knew what Kate's folks wanted for their daughter's future, and these young girls weren't going to be able to change those ideas.

She sighed and handed Kate her cloak. "Sometimes those that love us cause more hurt with the loving than they do with anger. You have to be forgiving, if you can."

Kate kissed Hannah lightly on the cheek. She had already forgiven her parents. She wished she could have had their understanding, but there was no time left to wait. She was not leaving to spite them, merely to save herself. As she hurried home in the cold morning air, she set her mind and heart to the future, and to Jessie.

Kate's head ached terribly and the house seemed intolerably warm as she hurried about gathering up the few clothes and personal treasures that she could not leave behind. Her father was at the newspaper office, and her mother was out to tea. It was the first chance she'd had to pack.

She had written a letter to her parents explaining what she had done, praying with each painful sentence that they would understand and someday believe that she was happy. She put the envelope on her bedside table, intending to leave it in the kitchen the next day for them to find. She wanted to get everything ready so that she could leave as soon as the house was empty in the morning.

Tomorrow was her mother's day to visit her new friends at the ladies' weekly luncheon gathering. *Tomorrow*, she thought, *tomorrow I will go to Jessie, and we will make a new life.*

It had only been twenty-four hours since they had parted, but she already missed Jessie terribly. Now, when things were so very hard, she needed her near. Jessie was always so calm, so steady. So strong.

When she thought of her leaving her beloved ranch, Kate's heart ached. She had only to envision her standing on the wide front porch looking contentedly out over her land, or astride one of her great horses, grinning and confidant and so totally at peace, to know what a great sacrifice Jessie was making. Kate hated for her to give up such a part of herself, but she could not imagine any other way. They could not stay, and Kate could not give her up. *If I lost Jessie, it would surely kill me.*

We must go.

Upstairs in her room, she opened her travel trunk, the one she had packed with such optimism less than a year before. She passed a trembling hand over her forehead, wiping with a handkerchief at the icy sweat that had broken out there. Then she felt suddenly cold. Shivering, she reached for a shawl. As she finished filling the suitcase, adding her slim book of sonnets to rest on top, she remembered sitting by Jessie's bedside reading them. The thought of Jessie warmed her even as her body grew more chilled.

She dragged the heavy valise toward her closet, suddenly feeling light-headed. She'd missed breakfast, being much too nervous to eat and could not recall now if she had even eaten dinner the night before. As the room started to tilt, she grasped the dresser for support. It was becoming more difficult by the moment to think clearly.

Frightened by the trembling in her limbs, she descended the staircase unsteadily and made her way to the kitchen. With one hand trailing along the wall, she struggled to stay upright. She found a pitcher of tea her mother had left in the heavy wooden icebox and carried it with shaking hands to the table. *A drink and some bread and honey is all I need.* Her vision wavering slightly, she laid the shawl aside, much too warm now.

As she reached for a glass, her head spun and a wave of nausea overtook her. She clutched the counter, her knees buckling. The room swirled. A curtain of gray obscured her vision, and she was dimly aware of the cool kitchen floor under her cheek. Barely conscious, too weak to rise, she called Jessie's name.

In short order, she lost all sense of time. At some point though, she was aware of being moved and of raised voices calling her name. She struggled weakly, protesting incoherently, as someone removed her clothing. She tried desperately to focus, knowing there was something she must do. Somewhere she must go. Eventually, her body surrendered to the fever, and she slipped into total unconsciousness with Jessie's name, now unspoken, on her lips.

Jessie paced the length of the porch, watching the dusk give way to darkness. A tarp-covered wagon stood waiting behind the house, packed with all they would need for their trip over the Rockies. Star and Rory were fed and bridled, ready for the journey as well. She stood at the rail, one arm braced along the porch post, staring toward the cookhouse. There were lights in the windows and the smell of stew in the air. Jed would be there, with the men. *God, it's hard, saying goodbye.*

Jed had said little when she told him she was leaving. He had stood quietly, chewing thoughtfully on a piece of hay, as Jessie explained that she would send legal papers giving him the authority to handle all the business affairs of the ranch. She thought at one point her voice would give out, but she held steady and looked him in the eye while she talked.

When she finished and fell silent, Jed had looked past her toward the mountains, as if gauging the climb. "You'll need to hurry if you're going to beat the snows," he said finally.

"Yes," she replied.

He had taken off his hat and brushed it lightly against his thigh. They were leaning against the corral fence, the two of them, hunched in their heavy jackets, eyes tearing faintly in the cold wind. "I know you ain't running from the law," he said.

"No."

"There are only two things I know that will make a man leave his home," Jed remarked quietly, his eyes still fixed on the distant hills. "The law or a woman."

She stiffened slightly, pushed her hands a little deeper in the pockets of her jacket. "Yes."

He looked back at her, and all he saw was the same clear gaze and steady strength he had always seen. "Ain't nothing you can do but leave?"

Sorrow swelled within her, the anger gone now. "No."

"Well," he said after another long pause. "When you feel you can come back, it will all still be here waitin'. I can assure you that."

"Jed, I...hell..."

"You'll be back. It's where you belong."

Her throat too tight to speak, she had only nodded. They had remained at the corral fence a while longer, their shoulders barely touching, watching the sky cloud over and the wind blow bare branches around the yard. She was glad for his company because it kept the sadness away.

That had been hours ago, and Kate was late. She should have arrived before sundown. Jessie looked up the road in the descending gloom for the hundredth time, even though she knew in her heart that Kate would have come by now if she were coming at all. Something must have happened. Perhaps she had been discovered.

A faint voice in the back of her mind kept whispering that maybe Kate had thought better about leaving and changed her mind—that she would have come had she wanted to. Perhaps at the final moment, she could not say goodbye. Too much risk, too much loss. Jessie could almost understand if that's what had happened. It would be harder for Kate than for her, leaving everything behind. Maybe what they shared wasn't enough, maybe...maybe...

"No," she growled under her breath, beginning to pace again. *I can't believe it.* She truly couldn't. She remembered Kate's eyes when she had declared that she loved her. She remembered Kate's touch, and her smile, and her soft sighs as they lay quietly wrapped in one another after loving. Of course Kate would come. She had said that she would. But the night said otherwise.

As midnight came and went, Jessie sat on the steps, weary from the hours of anxious waiting, elbows propped on her knees, her head down. She stared bleakly at nothing, her mind a blank. The star-filled sky revolved slowly overhead, and the night air drew down around her, but she remained motionless, impervious to the cold that slowly chilled her to the bone.

All the lights were out in the bunkhouses, and even the night seemed to sleep. She finally forced herself to move. Star and Rory still waited patiently, tied to the wagon, and she could not leave them unsheltered in the brutal wind for the rest of the night. Mechanically, she walked them down to the barn, removed their bridles, and led them into stalls. Then she made her way back up to the house, pausing on the porch to search the dark with desperate eyes, hoping to see deliverance emerge from the shadows. She swayed slightly and grasped the banister to steady herself. When she ran a hand over her face, she was surprised at the moisture on her cheeks. She couldn't feel anything, not even the tears. Then, very slowly, she turned her back to the road, walked into the house, and shut the door on hope.

CHAPTER NINETEEN

For four days, the terrible illness raged through New Hope. More than half the families in town were struck by the fast-moving influenza, and everyone had a friend or loved one down sick with the high fevers, wracking coughs, and suffocating bloody fluids in the lungs. In some homes, there were deaths, mostly among the very young or the very old—the ones with little strength to fight the rampaging infection. But here and there, it was a young man or woman, struck down suddenly, and taken within hours. Those who escaped the disease were afraid to leave their homes, and the streets lay eerily deserted. The few who were too restless or too stubborn to stay inside congregated at the saloon.

Frank had come down sick the previous day, and Mae and those of her girls who were still well were looking after the customers in the bar. Conversation was slight, most men lingering remorsefully over half-finished drinks, not wanting to talk of news that seemed all bad. Mae tried to keep up appearances, chatting briefly with each newcomer, forcing a smile. She stared in surprise at the newest face in the long row of unshaven men leaning against the bar. Thaddeus Schroeder nodded hello, his face drawn and pale.

"Thaddeus!" Mae said warmly, "Never expected to see you in here during daylight hours. Wish it was under better circumstances. What can I get you?"

Thaddeus smiled wanly. "A good strong whiskey, Mae. Things are getting terrible, just terrible."

Mae looked at him pityingly and poured him a drink. "How are your people?"

"My John Emory's ailing with it, but Doc said last night that the boy had passed the crisis, thank the good Lord. He wasn't sick at all just three days ago, and then…It comes so fast." He cleared his throat and reached for the glass that Mae pushed toward him. "Doc says we're lucky that we lived through that terrible spell in '52. Makes us stronger now."

She patted his hand. "That's fine, Thaddeus, just fine."

Mae had missed the terrible epidemic that swept over the western plains and beyond over a decade before, decimating the Indian populations and new settlers as well. But she had seen the effects of the devastating infection in the crowded tenements of New York City, and death looked the same everywhere. She prayed that this outbreak would be over quickly and the losses few. Lord, life was hard enough without this, too. "Maybe the worst has passed, then."

But Thaddeus was beyond consoling. He had come to the saloon because he needed to talk, and he couldn't burden his wife, who was so busy herself looking after the boy and helping the neighbors, too. He continued to ramble, almost to himself. "There are so many, Mae. So many others sick with it. More will die, God help us."

"Thaddeus," Mae said kindly, touching his hand again. "These people are strong, pioneer stock. They'll survive. Don't you be giving up hope now."

He raised remorseful eyes to hers. "It's Martin and Martha Beecher I feel so bad about. They're not like the rest of us, not used to such hardships. I feel like it's my fault for bringing them out here. That girl is going to be on my conscience, Mae." Tears brimmed in his eyes, and he reached quickly for his handkerchief.

Mae felt an awful fear crowding out her breath. "Thaddeus, what are you talking about?"

"Kate," he replied when he managed to contain himself. "She came down with the illness yesterday, and Doc says she's very bad. Might not even make it 'til tomorrow." He finished his drink. "My fault. All my fault."

Mae wanted to scream at him to hush so she could think. *Kate dying? That can't be, can it? Not young, beautiful, vibrant Kate. But of course it can.* There was no rhyme or reason to these things, and very little one could do to change fate. Not a thing, really.

She turned away from the stricken man, unable to summon any words of solace. Sadly, she moved down the bar, pouring shots of inadequate comfort for the mourners.

The house had a dark, deserted look about it. The windows were dead eyes staring back at her, and not even a breath of smoke curled from the chimney. For an instant, her heart seized with terror. What if death had visited here already? Would anyone have thought to tell her? Wouldn't she have known somehow if Jess were gone? Controlling her panic, Mae knocked on the wide front door. When there was no answer, she pushed it open and hesitantly stepped into the hall. It was beyond cold inside, as if all life had indeed departed days before.

"Who is it?" a low, quiet voice said out of the darkness.

Mae cried out sharply, searching the darkness in the direction of the voice. "Jess? For God's sake, Jess, is that you?"

A match flared, flickered, and then caught. A moment later lamplight illuminated the adjacent room and Mae followed the faint yellow glow. Jessie stood wraith-like by the fireplace, pale and hollow-eyed. She placed the lamp on the mantle and turned slowly toward Mae, her normally straight back slumped, her gaze dazed and listless.

"What is it, Mae?" She gripped the edge of the stone ledge tightly, a little unsteady on her feet. She hadn't had much to eat. Couldn't remember her last meal actually.

The fireplace was empty; she hadn't cooked. She dimly recalled Jed coming up to the house that morning, or maybe it was the night before, asking after her. He was saying he had seen the wagon still out back, warning that the snows were coming any day. She had sent him away, telling him she wouldn't be needing the wagon after all. He had wanted to say more, she could see the worry in his face, but she had shut the door. There was nothing to say.

Jessie looked up from the cold hearth, surprised to see Mae still standing there, staring at her. She cleared her throat. "What is it?" she asked again.

Mae came forward slowly, wondering if Jessie was sick with what everyone else had. She looked so drained, so empty. Mae had never seen her look like this, not even right after her father had been killed. "Jess, are you sick?"

"No." She didn't feel sick. She didn't feel anything. Just a strange kind of numbness everywhere. She guessed that's all there would ever be.

"Then what are you doing in here in the dark?" Mae was so worried and so scared she was beginning to lose her temper. "It's freezing in here, too! Are you *trying* to get sick?"

The hard edge in Mae's voice penetrated Jessie's muddled consciousness. "I'm not sick," she said, a little of the life returning to her voice. "What are you talking about? Why do you keep asking that? Why are you here?"

Mae gasped. "Lord, you don't know, do you?"

"Know what?" Jessie asked, an ominous dread stirring in her chest. "What's happening?"

"The grippe," Mae said bitterly. "It hit town a bit ago, and the last two days have seen some sorrow."

Slowly, Jessie's face lost its last trace of color. "Kate," she whispered. *God, I am such a fool! Why didn't I go into town and look for her? How could I let my doubts keep me away?* She grabbed Mae's shoulders. "Kate! Is she sick?"

Mae paused, not sure until just that moment what she had come to say. The torment and terror in Jessie's face convinced her. She said very quietly, "She's bad, Jess. Doc says she doesn't have long."

Jessie's head snapped back as if Mae had struck her. For a moment, she was completely still, the only movement a faint pulse beating in her neck. Then a horrible glint flashed in her eyes and a sound more like a snarl than a word tore from her throat.

"No!"

Mae caught Jessie's arm as she snatched her gun belt from the table and strapped it on. "Jess," she said hesitantly, afraid of what she might do in her state of mind. "Her family—"

The look Jessie gave her stopped Mae cold.

"There's not a man alive can keep me from her, Mae," Jessie answered stonily and headed for the door. "I can't let her die without me there."

Martha was jolted from an uneasy slumber by a commotion downstairs. She had been restlessly napping in the small sitting room adjoining Kate's bedroom while Hannah kept watch. Martin had retired to his library hours before, too distraught to sit vigil at his daughter's bedside. Hannah came into the room just as Martha hastily retied the laces on her bodice.

"Whoever is at the door?" Martha asked impatiently. "They'll disturb Kate!"

Hannah regarded Martha sympathetically, not mentioning that Kate had not been aware of anything for some time. Martha's hair was falling from its pins, her eyes were hollow, and her face gaunt. *Poor woman*, Hannah thought, and whispered a quick prayer of thanks that her own son was on the mend. She'd only just that evening been able to leave John Emory's bedside. Knowing that Martha would need help looking after Kate, she'd come straight away and immediately sent Martha off for some much needed rest. "It's Jessie Forbes."

Martha stared uncomprehendingly, her confusion quickly turning to alarm. "Here? She's here?"

"Seems so." Hannah wasn't surprised by Martha's look of distress. Even though she and Martha had had no chance to talk about any of the events of the last few days, she'd suspected trouble when Jessie had shown up at her house unannounced. She'd figured then that Martin and Martha had gotten wind of what was happening between the two girls, and there was only one way *that* could end.

"Why has she come?" Martha repeated distractedly. "Why now, of all times?"

"I expect she wants to see Kate." When she first heard the pounding on the front door, she'd been afraid that it might have been Thaddeus come to say that John Emory had taken poorly again. She'd gone to the top of the landing to see who was there and saw Jessie Forbes standing in the doorway. Martin was blocking her way, and it'd looked from Jessie's expression like she might shoot him. "Appears to be set on it."

"Impossible," Martha said firmly.

"I don't think she's going to go away, Martha."

"No, I suppose not," Martha said in a strange voice, amazed at the strength of the bond between her daughter and this unusual young woman. She slipped her hand into the pocket of the apron she wore and handed a folded paper to Hannah. "I found this on Kate's bedside table yesterday."

Hannah carefully unfolded the much-read note and studied the message written there. *Oh Lord,* she thought as she read. *Poor Kate.*

When she finished, she slowly handed it back to Martha. She wasn't sure what to say, so she waited for Martha to speak.

"Kate was going to run away," Martha said, clearly still shocked by the idea. She looked at Hannah with eyes filled with weariness and pain. "Can you imagine? She was simply going to disappear somewhere with that—woman."

"Seems they care for one another," Hannah said carefully.

"But to just leave us like that! Kate must have been ill, not thinking clearly." She didn't sound convinced even by her own words.

"Kate has a sound head on her, Martha. She left that note because she loves you and Martin. She didn't want you to worry too much."

"You're not saying that you approve, are you?" Martha's astonishment was clear.

"It's not for me to approve or disapprove. But it appears that Kate knows her own mind." With a faint smile she added, "Can't imagine where she gets *that* stubborn streak from."

"So, you think that we should encourage this madness? That I should allow that young woman to see Kate?" Martha asked defensively. *Oh, if only we had never left Boston!*

"Martha," Hannah said quietly, "I lost my three youngest in the epidemic of '52. It's a sorrow you never get over, burying a child." She saw the expression of pain and fright in Martha's face and regretted causing it, but she continued on, fearing Kate's loss more than Martha's anger. "Love has strange power. I've even known it to heal. If Jessie Forbes can keep Kate with you, I'd surely say pride had no place in the matter."

Martha was silent, her gaze moving to the still figure in the other room. Kate had barely been conscious the last twelve hours, and when she had managed any words at all, she had whispered Jessie's name. *Hannah is right. If there is any chance under heaven that this young woman can make a difference—well, I'll worry about the rest of it later.* She turned determinedly toward the stairs. "Thank you, Hannah," she murmured as she hurried past.

Jessie faced Martin in the doorway. She was very close to doing harm. "I *have* to see her," she repeated, her voice dangerously low.

Martin continued to stand in her way, his grief overpowering all other thought. He knew that Kate had planned to run away and leave them, and now she might truly leave them. Forever.

"Kate is going to die in peace!" he shouted, seeking any object upon which to vent his rage at this monstrous injustice.

"No." Jessie passed a quivering hand over her eyes, unable to bear his words. "Please. Just let me see her."

"Why?" he asked harshly. "What can you do?"

"I love her. Please, I—"

"Get out."

She could bear the agony no longer. She would not let Kate go this way. She could not. Reaching reflexively for her revolver, she took one step closer. "Move out of my way or I swear, I'll kill you!"

From behind them, Martha gasped, uncertain from the look on Jessie's face whether she meant to shoot Martin or herself. "Stop this, both of you! Carrying on this way with Kate lying sick upstairs. It's disgraceful."

"This is not for you to say," Martin said. "Go back upstairs."

Martha descended the last few steps and grasped her husband's arm. "Let her go to Kate. What harm can it do now?"

Jessie was already past them, taking the stairs two at a time. She slowed when she saw Hannah standing in the open doorway. "Kate?"

"In here," Hannah motioned. "She's waiting for you."

"Thank you." Jessie stepped quietly into a dimly lit room and found her breath suddenly short. The dank, heavy air added to her choking dread, and she scarcely registered the valise standing open by the closet, nor anything about the room other than the slight figure in the bed. Her heart hammered so hard in her chest she thought this sound alone might awaken Kate.

There was an eerie stillness about the way Kate lay motionless, eyes closed, face ashen and glistening with sweat. The bedcovers barely rose with each shallow, labored breath. Jessie knelt next to her and reached out with trembling fingers to gently stroke the pallid cheek.

"Kate," she murmured, the word a faint cry. She closed her eyes for a moment, trying to steady herself, then spoke again, her voice stronger. "Kate, love. It's Jessie." She pressed her lips to Kate's hot palm, her own warm tears landing softly on the fragile skin. "Love, can you hear me?"

After what seemed a very long time and with tremendous effort, Kate's lids flickered open, and her gaze rested feverishly on Jessie's face. "Jessie?"

Jessie rejoiced. Kate was not gone, and she would *not* let her go. "Yes, love. I'm here."

"I…tried…to come." She wanted so much for Jessie to know that.

"I know. I know you did." Jessie felt like she was drowning. She clung to the limp fingers, willing strength into them. "And when you are well again, we will be together always. I promise you, Kate. I promise." She struggled not to crumble. Her voice broke. "Please, Kate. I need you so."

Kate's eyes were suddenly quite clear and very calm. She smiled at Jessie, and her voice held an odd note of peace. "I won't be going away with you, Jessie darling. You must be without me for a while."

"No, Kate. No!" Jessie shook, her body wracked with sobs. "You *will* be well again."

"Jessie…my only love." Kate raised her hand to Jessie's tear-streaked face. "You must say goodbye."

"I can't. I can't. Oh Lord, Kate, please don't go." Jessie leaned forward, but Kate's eyes were closing. "Kate!"

Martha Beecher, watching from the hall, stifled a sob and turned away as Jessie pressed her lips to Kate's. This moment was not hers to witness.

CHAPTER TWENTY

A s the darkest hours of night enshrouded the Beecher home, Martha returned from comforting her husband to Kate's room. She entered silently, then halted at the sound of soft words murmured in quiet desperation. Jessie was still on her knees at the bedside, her head bowed over Kate's still figure, clasping Kate's hand in both of hers. Her voice cracked with anguish.

"Kate," she implored, sure that somehow, somewhere, Kate heard her. "I love you. Oh Lord, Kate, I love you with every breath. I don't know how I'll..." She brushed at the tears that fell again, drawing a shaky breath. She couldn't let Kate die being worried for her. She straightened her shoulders, but with each word, it felt like a bit of her was dying, too. "It will be all right, Kate. You needn't fear for me. I will never leave you, I swear. I will wait here for you, or hereafter, however long it need be. I am here, always, love."

Martha placed her hand gently on Jessie's trembling shoulder, shocked at her frailty. Her hard strength seemed to have dissolved as Kate's life slipped away. "Jessie," she murmured, her anger and suspicion disappearing in the face of such torment. "Let it go, child. The Lord will do His bidding."

Jessie turned in mute despair, her face filled with unspeakable anguish. An agonized cry tore from her chest, and she doubled over.

Stunned at the depth of her desolation, Martha instinctively reached out to comfort a suffering soul. She knelt and wrapped Jessie in her arms. Holding her to her bosom, she rocked her while she cried and stroked her damp face with tender fingers. "Shh, now. You mustn't let her hear you cry. You must be strong now, Jessie. For Kate."

At last, Jessie's sobs stilled and Martha led her stumbling and dazed to a chair by the window. "Wait here. We will know by morning."

Jessie bowed her head and covered her face with her hands.

Martha dragged a chair to Kate's bedside. Absently, she reached for the thin leather volume that she had found in Kate's valise. The book fell open to a well-read page, and she picked up the photo marking the place. In the dim light of the oil lamp, she could see that Jessie had been smiling at Kate when Kate took the photograph. There was a carefree exuberance about her that made Martha's heart ache. *They're both so young.*

For a moment she forgot that they were two young women, seeing only the love she could not deny. She began to read the poem that Kate had marked with Jessie's photograph.

> *So are you to my thoughts as food to life,*
> *Or as sweet-season'd showers are to the ground;*
> *And for the peace of you I hold such strife…*

Tears blurred her vision, and she could not go on, feeling as if she had trodden upon some sacred place. She looked from Kate's fragile countenance to Jessie's haunted face and prayed for them both. As the hours passed, she watched Kate's fever consume her, visibly draining the last reserves of strength from her weakened body. Her breathing grew more and more labored, and finally Martha rose to find her husband, fearing that it might already be too late for him to say goodbye. She met Jessie's eyes as she crossed to the door and had to look away from the agony she saw there. She had not thought it possible that anyone, man or woman, could love so unreservedly as that.

Jessie stood by the window looking out into blackness, her back to the room, her face veiled in shadows. She did not turn when Martha and Martin entered just before dawn, knowing what they would find. She had heard when the faint arduous struggles of Kate's uneven breathing had stopped, and in that instant, a darkness deeper than night had fallen over her world. It would remain there, she knew, forever.

Martha's muffled cry, and Martin's faint groan, pierced her heart, and she closed her eyes. She could not bear knowing Kate was gone, even if it might be to some better place. For that she fervently hoped, but it gave her no comfort as the first terrible anguish of loss ripped through her.

In a moment, she thought, *in a moment I will go and leave them with their daughter and their grief.* She kept one hand braced tightly on the windowsill, uncertain that her legs would carry her from the room. She trembled uncontrollably, and she struggled to see through her tears.

"Martin!" Martha cried.

"Oh Kate," Jessie whispered in desperation.

"Is she gone?" Martin groaned.

I love you, Kate, Jessie thought, forcing herself to turn, wanting to see her, not knowing how she would say goodbye.

Martha stood with her hand resting on Kate's cheek, boundless joy on her face. "Her face is cool! The fever has broken. She is only sleeping!"

Jessie sank into the chair and wept.

Seated by the bed, Jessie held Kate's hand in hers, watching her sleep peacefully. She heard Martha return from speaking with the doctor and brushed her lips over the open palm, then laid Kate's hand gently down upon her breast. She rose to face Martha, fearful of the news.

"What did he say?"

"That it will probably be a long convalescence, but there's good reason to hope she will recover fully." Martha stood just inside Kate's bedroom door. For some reason, she felt as if she were intruding on something intensely personal every time she looked at Jessie looking at her daughter. There was nothing unseemly about it; only something so intimate, it made her uncomfortable. She hadn't imagined even a man and a woman could share such feeling.

"I'll be going now," Jessie said softly. She could barely manage the words. She was worn beyond exhaustion. Empty.

Martha gazed from Jessie's tortured eyes to Kate, deep in healing sleep. She said nothing. It was best—at least it would be in time—if this could end now.

"Will you tell her I was here?" Jessie asked, brushing sweat from her face with a trembling hand. "Please?"

"I think it would be best if I didn't."

The words struck like a blow, and Jessie's eyes flickered closed for a moment. She steadied herself with one hand on the edge of the bedside table. When she recovered her breath, she met Martha's gaze directly. "Would it? Is hurting her ever for the best?"

Martha looked away, remembering the words Kate had written in the farewell letter. *"I love her, more than I will ever love anyone else in my life. I need to be with her, or my life will not be worth living."* Surely, surely, Kate could not have meant that.

"What would you give to make her happy?" Martha asked suddenly.

"Anything," Jessie answered immediately.

"Then go, leave her. Leave Kate to live the life she should." The words were spoken pleadingly, with no anger. Martha had seen enough to know that there was no sin between them, only an ill-advised affection. Women were not meant to live for passion, or even happiness, but to do their duty. Kate would simply have to accept that.

"Mrs. Beecher," Jessie said steadily, mustering all the strength she had left. "If Kate tells me to go, I swear to you that I will never see her again."

"And if she does not?"

"Then there is nothing and no one who will keep me from her. If you send her away, I will find her. I promised her that I would never stop loving her." She looked one last time at Kate and then slowly walked past Martha toward the stairs. "I meant it."

CHAPTER TWENTY-ONE

A steady rapping on the door awakened Jessie. She looked around the room, trying to figure out where she was and how she got here. She was on a bed, still in her clothes, her hat and gun belt on the chair nearby. Her head ached and her stomach was queasy. She turned toward the window. It looked like it was late in the day, and as she struggled to orient herself, the rapping came again.

"Come in," she croaked and swung her legs over the side of the bed. She didn't feel steady enough to stand just yet.

Mae came in carrying coffee and toast on a tray, and Jessie could have kissed her. She sat down on the bed next to Jessie and set the tray between them. "Well, you look a mite better than this morning, but not by much. Drink some of that. You need it."

"Lord, that smells good." Jessie reached for the steaming cup, vaguely recalling that she had stumbled into the hotel just after dawn. She remembered Mae's arm around her waist, helping her up the stairs. And Mae laying her down, and starting to unbutton her shirt.

"Thanks," Jessie said at length. "For last night—this morning, I mean."

"How are you?" Mae asked. It didn't seem to her that the sleep had done Jessie much good. Her eyes were darkly shadowed, her face drawn and etched with pain. She didn't look quite as wild as when Mae had seen her out at the ranch, but she was still far from right. "How's Kate?"

A faint light of happiness flared in Jessie's eyes. "She's better, Doc says…" She faltered, her throat suddenly tight. "Doc says she will get well."

Mae put her hand gently on Jessie's arm. "That's fine, Jess," she said, meaning it. "That's fine."

"Yes." Jessie sipped some more coffee and stood wearily. "I should get back to the ranch."

"You should lay back down and sleep for two days," Mae said roughly, moving to stop her from reaching for her gun belt. "You're in no shape to ride. You look like a good wind could blow you away. You need rest, or you'll be sick abed, too, and no good to anyone, least of all Kate."

"Kate?" Jessie asked dumbly. She was having a very hard time making sense of anything anymore. Just a few days ago, she had been set to leave behind everything she had ever known so that she might have a life with Kate. Then she'd believed that Kate had abandoned their dream. She'd slipped into a nightmare of despair, only to awaken to find Kate dying. That terror haunted her still. She had no idea what to do next. "I...Kate?"

"You don't think you're the first person she'll want to see when she wakes up?" Mae asked with exasperation. "You're going to need all your wits to handle that family, and she's going to need you to be strong."

"What if they won't let me see her?" Jessie asked, her voice low and tortured. Lord, she was tired, and her mind was so muddled.

Mae cursed her own stupidity. *Why am I always taking Kate's side in all of this? Why didn't I just ignore Jessie's protests and finish undressing her this morning? I should have just crawled into that bed next to her the way I've been wanting to do for years, and maybe then Jessie would have given up this damn fool idea of being with Kate Beecher.* She looked at Jessie and knew why she had done none of those things. Jessie loved Kate, and there was no changing it. She sighed.

"Montana, I don't believe there's a man alive who could stop you from doin' something if you set your mind to it. You said so yourself just a bit ago. Once you get some sleep, you'll know what to do."

She put her arm around Jessie's shoulders and directed her back to the bed. Jessie raised no objection, and even let Mae remove her shirt and pants, smiling faintly when Mae leaned down and kissed her lightly, chastely, on the mouth. She was already asleep again by the time Mae gently closed the door.

❖

Kate roused in the still room to the sound of pages quietly turning. She was very weak, but there was no pain. In fact, she felt very calm, serene. After a moment, she moved her head on the pillow.

"Mother," she whispered.

"Oh!" Martha dropped her book in her haste to reach Kate's side. "Oh, Kate. We were so worried."

"I'm sorry."

"Hush," Martha chided, gently brushing Kate's hair back from her face. "I'll get your father. He's still asleep."

"Wait." Kate seized her mother's hand. "Where's Jessie?"

Martha hesitated, then answered truthfully. "I don't know."

Kate's expression darkened. "Is she all right? She isn't ill, is she?"

"Not that I know of. Don't upset yourself. You need to worry about getting well. Nothing else."

"No, I need to see her. If I'm asleep when she comes, be sure to wake me."

"When she comes?" Martha asked in surprise.

"She'll come, as soon as she's able." Kate's smile was fleeting, but sure. "I know that she was here. I can remember her voice. Her hands." She saw her mother's expression grow cold. "You found the note, didn't you?"

Martha dropped her eyes. "We can talk about that later."

"There's nothing to talk about," Kate said faintly, suddenly very tired. "I will never change my mind. No matter what we must do, where we must go…"

"Oh, Kate," Martha sighed as her daughter gave in to sleep. She despaired of ever changing Kate's mind. And if she couldn't, then what was she to do? *We cannot force her into marriage, and if we send her east, what then? Will that be enough to keep them apart?* She remembered the determination on Jessie Forbes's face and the certainty in Kate's eyes. *No, I do not think so.*

She had almost lost Kate to death, and the unthinkable agony of that near loss lingered in her mind. Kate had been returned to her, a gift. She would surely lose her, she realized, if she tried to stand in their way, and that thought was more unbearable than anything else. She recalled Hannah's words: *Love has strange power. If Jessie Forbes can keep Kate with you...* She leaned down and kissed Kate's cool forehead, whispering a prayer of thanks for her child's life.

❖

Jessie unconsciously straightened her shoulders as Martin Beecher opened the door. He stood looking at her for a long moment, as if making a decision. He looked years older, and Jessie figured she didn't look a whole lot better herself. She had slept one entire day through, and when she had awakened, she found her shirt and pants cleaned and waiting by the bedside. She had dressed hastily and come straight to the Beechers'. Now, she waited for him to say whatever he needed to say. She was calm, resolute. Only Kate could send her away.

"Jessie."

"Mr. Beecher. I've come to see Kate."

Martin stepped out onto the porch and closed the door. He searched his pockets for a cigar as he walked to the rail. It was starting to snow, and the air was very cold. He snipped off the end of the cigar and lit it as Jessie came to stand beside him.

"Strange country, this," he said at last. "So beautiful, but so deadly."

"Is it so different, back in Boston?"

Martin watched the smoke from his cigar drift upward. "Not so beautiful. Maybe just as deadly, but it more often kills the spirit than the body."

Jessie nodded, thinking there couldn't be anything much worse than dying inside while you were still walking around. The way she had felt when Kate was sick. "How is Kate?"

"She's very weak, and she'll need a long rest. The doctor said another episode like this one could be dangerous. But by spring, he said, she should be fine."

Spring. Five months. Some of the tension left Jessie's body.

"Is it true, what she says?" Martin Beecher asked, his voice low, his eyes fixed on the faraway mountain peaks. "That you love her?"

"Yes," Jessie answered without a second's hesitation.

"She says that the two of you will go away, west somewhere, if we try to prevent her from living with you at the ranch." He spoke as if the words were foreign to him, bewilderment in his tone and expression.

"Yes."

"You'd do that? Give up everything for her?"

"I'd have given my life upstairs in trade for hers if I could have."

"Yes, so would I." Finally, he met her gaze directly. "Will you promise me something?"

She waited.

"Will you promise to care for her always?"

We will care for each other, she thought, but she understood what he was asking. "With my last breath."

"And you will not take her away from us."

"I would never want to do that. Kate loves you."

Martin sighed tiredly. "Then I'll not keep you from her. I will not lose her to pride."

Jessie felt suddenly dizzy as a great weight was lifted from her heart. She drew a deep breath and then another, finally feeling the strength return to her limbs. "I'd like to see her now."

"She's waiting." He did not turn as Jessie walked into the house.

Kate pushed up in bed, her heart swelling with joy, as Jessie came toward her. She frowned just a little when she saw the dark smudges under Jessie's normally clear eyes. Then Jessie was leaning down to kiss her, and she forgot everything except her soft lips on her mouth.

After a long moment, Jessie stepped back and smiled. "Kate."

"Hello, my darling." Kate tugged her by the hand down onto the bed next to her. She rested her head on Jessie's shoulder, wrapped an arm around her waist, and sighed contentedly.

Jessie pressed her lips to Kate's temple. "Your mother is likely to come up here. She saw me on my way inside." Martha's greeting had been surprisingly calm. There had been something close to acceptance in her eyes.

"No, she won't bother us this time." Kate held Jessie tighter. "In the future, we may very well have a chaperone while I am under my parent's roof, but not today. She knows how much I need you here now."

"Lord, I love you," Jessie whispered, gently stroking her cheek. "I'm not right when you're not with me."

"I'll be with you soon. Forever."

Jessie kissed her softly. "When you're well, you'll come to the ranch to live with me."

"Yes," Kate answered, drawing strength from Jessie's presence. "It won't be long."

Jessie hesitated, remembering the doctor's warning about Kate's still-fragile health. Winters at the ranch were the hardest season of the year. She often couldn't get into town for weeks because of high snows and frigid temperatures. She couldn't risk Kate falling sick again that far from medical care. "You need time to recover, Kate. And winter has come. You should stay here until spring."

Kate raised herself enough to look into Jessie's face, wondering how Jessie could so easily accept such a separation. "Do you imagine that I could stand to be away from you for five months?"

"It's not so long," Jessie insisted valiantly, though the vision of endless days and nights without Kate made her despair.

"No?" Her hand slid slowly over Jessie's chest, lingering over the soft swell of her breast, teasing until she felt her nipple harden through the cotton shirt. "You'll not notice my absence?"

Jessie's eyes widened, the pupils growing dark. "Lord, Kate. Don't." She caught Kate's hand to still her teasing, trying desperately to ignore the pounding that had started in her belly from just that brief caress. "I want you so much from just being here next to you. You'll kill me if you do that."

"Then don't make me wait all winter," Kate threatened, but she settled back into the crook of Jessie's arm, too tired yet to do more.

Drawing a ragged breath, Jessie thanked the Lord that Kate didn't know how near she was to losing all hold of herself. "I'll be gone almost two months before the roundup, up in the mountains with the men," she managed to say. "Won't get down to the ranch but for a few days here or there."

"I know you're speaking sense." Kate could barely stand and would be no help at all on the ranch. *But so long!* She couldn't imagine being without Jessie's sweet touch all that time. "We'll have little chance to be alone," she warned, "if I stay here."

"And don't think I won't be suffering." Jessie raised Kate's chin with her fingers and looked deeply into her eyes. She longed for Kate's reassuring touch to banish her fears and the memory of nearly losing her. "I need you, Kate. I need you to love me, the way we do when we're alone. Lord, how I need that. But I need you well and with me more than anything else." She closed her eyes against the fierce wanting.

Kate read the need in her face and heard the yearning in her voice. "Jessie," she whispered, aching to ease those longings. "I love you."

Jessie smiled and blew out a shaky breath. "Well, I guess I can wait a while for the rest."

Snuggling closer, Kate closed her eyes, exhausted. As she fell asleep, she made a silent vow. *I might have to wait five months to live with you, but I won't be waiting that long to love you again.*

CHAPTER TWENTY-TWO

The people of New Hope slowly resumed their lives in the aftermath of the illness, but for many, the struggles brought changes and a renewed sense of appreciation for each day's gifts. Martin Beecher, for one, now spent lunchtimes at home, basking in the sound of Kate's soft laughter as she recovered. Never had life seemed so precious.

Kate grew stronger day by day, as content as she could be waiting for the times when Jessie managed to come in from the ranch to spend an afternoon with her. With Martha or both parents in attendance during their visits, they never had time to speak of their love. Still, they shared devotions with a glance and made promises on a smile, the brief touch of fingers and the fleeting brush of lips their only caress.

As hard as it was to be near Jessie and not be able to touch her as she so desperately wanted, Kate found it harder still to be separated from her. Each time they parted at the door, Jessie would lean near and whisper, "I love you, Kate," and those words sustained her, nourished her, and gave her hope.

Finally, roundup week arrived again, and Jessie brought her herd into town for auction. As soon as Jessie's business was finished, Kate planned to return with her to the Rising Star. The week was as hectic as it had been the year before, and most of the time Kate had to content herself with watching her lover from a distance. The anticipation of seeing her, and knowing that soon she would be with her, always, was sweet in a way she hadn't expected.

Now that it was only a matter of days, she could look at her and dream of her touch with delight. When Jessie caught her eye in the crowd or tipped her hat across the corral, a soft smile lighting her face, Kate's heart tripped over itself. *Soon*, she whispered, *soon*.

At last, the waiting was nearly over. The next day would see an end to the auction for another year. Martin had gone out with Thaddeus to put the finishing touches on the newspaper, and Kate sat with Martha on the porch, listening to the faraway sounds of cattle lowing and men laughing. *Jessie is out there somewhere.* She closed her eyes, missing her. *Soon*, she thought again.

Martha sighed, mistaking her wistful look for sadness. "Are you sorry, Kate, that we came here?"

"Oh no! I love it here. I feel as if this is where I was always meant to be." Cautiously, she added, "And if we hadn't come, I would not have found Jessie." She saw her mother stiffen slightly and waited for the words she had been expecting for weeks.

"Are you quite sure about this?" Martha asked, even though there was very little time left to change her daughter's mind. She had seen the valises standing packed and ready in Kate's room. "Life will not be easy. Not at all what I had wished for you."

"Tell me, Mother, what is it you had wished for me?"

Martha sighed again, searching for dreams long past. "You are my only child. I wanted everything for you—security, a fine home—the things that would make you happy."

"And love?"

"If it were possible."

Kate smiled tenderly, her eyes glowing with the vision of Jessie. "Will you believe me, then, when I tell you that I will have all of those things, and more, with Jessie? She is all I want. All I ever dreamed of."

"You have made your choice, Kate," Martha said with quiet resignation. "I know that now. I do not pretend to understand it, but I cannot help but believe you. I have seen her look at you and you at her. I know what love looks like."

"I hope someday that you will be happy for me," Kate replied softly, reaching for her mother's hand.

"In time, Kate. In time."

❖

Jessie stood toweling the water from her hair when a knock sounded at her door. Just an hour before, she had finally concluded her business, paid her men their wages, and returned to the hotel to get cleaned up. She pulled the door open and stared in surprise.

"Kate!"

Kate delighted in her astonishment. "Hello, Jessie darling."

"I didn't expect you!"

"I know." Kate pulled the door closed, untied her bonnet, and placed it on the small dresser. She leaned back against the bureau, content just to look at Jessie. Barefoot, she wore a clean white cotton shirt and denim pants, and her deep blue eyes were already hazy with desire. Kate thought she had never seen her look so beautiful. "I have been waiting patiently all week for you."

The teasing tone in Kate's voice set Jessie's heart to hammering. She was incapable of forming any thoughts beyond wanting Kate. It was the first time in five months that they had been alone together.

"Kate," Jessie repeated, whispering now. She closed the distance between them, unable to take her eyes from Kate's, knowing that her need was plain on her face. She slid her hands to Kate's waist and sighed as Kate stepped into her arms. "Oh Lord, I've been wanting you so much. Every day. So much."

When Kate lifted her face, Jessie's lips were there. She pulled Kate tighter, gasping at the first sweet pressure of Kate's breasts against hers. Tenderly at first, with soft caresses and gentle murmurs, they welcomed one another. They trembled together, barely breathing, amazed at finally being able to touch. But it had been too long and their wanting was too great to join gently. Jessie groaned, her body aflame, and she pulled frantically at the ties on Kate's dress. She could not bear to lift her lips from Kate's, but yanked roughly at the barriers between them, her tongue moving over and into Kate's mouth.

Kate made small urgent cries in the back of her throat. Her fingers found Jessie's pants and tugged at the buttons, desperate for the feel of her.

"Wait, Kate!" Gasping, Jessie jerked her head back, shivering with need. "Help me get your clothes off. I can't manage it."

Kate laughed and began to unlace her bodice hurriedly. "You, too," she said, "those buttons are contrary."

They watched each other, breath held in anticipation as each piece of clothing fell to the floor. Jessie fumbled at the buttons on her shirt as she lowered her gaze to Kate's breasts, captivated by the faint blush of her skin and the tempting tautness of her nipples. She abandoned her attempts to unbutton her shirt and pulled it off over her head, then hurriedly pushed her pants off. Naked, she stepped forward, intent on having Kate's breasts in her hands.

Kate followed her gaze. "Oh no, not yet."

Jessie stopped abruptly, her eyes glazed. "What...Kate..."

Laughing, Kate stepped around her toward the bed. "If you put your hands on me, it will be over far too soon."

"I don't think I can wait," Jessie groaned, turning to follow.

"Just a minute," Kate murmured, nearly lost to Jessie's need. She drew down the covers on the bed and slipped underneath. "I've waited far too long for this." She held out her hand, her face glowing, and said softly, "Come love me slowly, Jessie Forbes."

Jessie hesitated by the side of the bed, her hands trembling. She whispered shakily, "I want you so badly, it scares me."

"It doesn't frighten me," Kate responded thickly, beginning to feel the urgency deep inside. Despite her intentions not to hurry, she craved Jessie's touch. "You could never frighten me."

Carefully, Jessie leaned down, pulling the sheet away with one hand. As her lips touched Kate's, she lightly stroked Kate's cheek, then along her neck to her chest. She ran her palm over Kate's breast, swollen now with arousal, and finally caught the nipple between her fingers. Kate moaned with the swift stab of pleasure, almost a sob, and Jessie shuddered at the sound. "I need you. I need you."

Kate clutched her shoulders, her fingers digging into the muscles she loved. "Lie with me."

Quickly, she settled upon her, sliding her thigh firmly between Kate's legs, moaning at the wetness that spread over her skin. She braced herself on her arms, and, looking down into Kate's face, rocked against her, her breath suspended as her blood rose high.

"Next time," Jessie gasped, feeling the pressure boiling up within her and the tension rippling down her legs. "Next time will be slow. This time, I can't wait."

"Neither can I." Kate exulted as she watched Jessie's face dissolve with need.

She clasped Jessie's hips and pushed harder against her thigh, each thrust bringing each closer to release. Her vision began to dim as her muscles vibrated on the verge of exploding. Back arched, she desperately tried to contain the uncontainable, and lost. "Oh…Jessie!"

With a strangled groan, Jessie's head snapped back, Kate's cry pushing her beyond her last vestige of restraint. Her arms trembled, her hips jerked violently, and, finally, she could do nothing but surrender.

"Kate," Jessie murmured drowsily when she came to her senses.

"Hmm?" Kate softly stroked Jessie's neck and back.

"It's late." With a sigh, she rolled away until she lay on her back, fingers loosely clasped in Kate's. "You'll need to be getting back."

Kate sat up reluctantly, pushing her hair away from her face with both hands. "I know. My mother is expecting me to help her get food ready for the dance." She regarded Jessie tenderly. "You *will* be there, won't you?"

Jessie smiled, remembering Kate asking her the same question a year ago. This time, she answered first with a kiss, and then said, "That's where you're going to be, isn't it?"

Kate smiled at the wrangler who stood patiently at the food table waiting for her to fill his plate with chicken and potatoes. She had been so busy with the endless stream of people that she'd had barely a chance to search for Jessie. It seemed that everyone in the meetinghouse wanted to inquire after her health and tell her how glad they were to see her up and about. Even Ken Turner, squiring a pretty young woman on his arm, had greeted her politely, though he hadn't lingered long. He had quickly stopped attending her during her convalescence when she had resolutely, in no uncertain terms, declined his offer of marriage.

Thankfully, the fiddlers were now beginning to play, and people were moving away to dance. She wiped her hands on a towel and made her way through the crowds out onto the back porch for some respite. She wasn't tired, but she was weary of making conversation. It didn't matter how well meaning her friends and acquaintances were. There was only one person she wanted to see.

The spring nights were still cool, but she welcomed the crisp, refreshing air. She gazed up at the dark night sky, punctuated by bright stars, and thought that at this time tomorrow, she would be standing on the porch of her new home. Smiling to herself, imagining the joy of lying in Jessie's arms at night, every night, she heard the jingle of spurs on the wood planks behind her. She did not turn, but savored the memory of the first time she had seen her beloved and heard the jingle of her spurs.

"What are you thinking?" Jessie asked softly as she stepped up behind Kate and rested her hands lightly on Kate's shoulders.

"Of going home with you." Kate settled back into Jessie's embrace with a contented smile.

Jessie brushed a kiss into Kate's hair. "Are you happy?"

Kate turned in the circle of Jessie's arms and clasped her hands loosely behind Jessie's neck. "There's no word beautiful enough for what I am," she whispered. "I am loved. I love. I have everything I ever wanted."

"So do I." Jessie kissed her gently. *Everything and more.*

There in the moonlight, with music whispering on the wind, they danced.

About the Author

Radclyffe is the author of numerous lesbian romances (*Safe Harbor* and its sequels *Beyond the Breakwater* and *Distant Shores, Silent Thunder*; *Love's Melody Lost, Love's Tender Warriors, Tomorrow's Promise, Passion's Bright Fury, Love's Masquerade, shadowland,* and *Fated Love*), two romance/intrigue series: the Honor series (*Above All, Honor, Honor Bound, Love & Honor, Honor Guards*) and the Justice series (*Shield of Justice,* the prequel *A Matter of Trust, In Pursuit of Justice, Justice in the Shadows,* and *Justice Served*), and selections in numerous erotica anthologies (*Erotic Interludes 1 and 2* from Bold Strokes Books, *After Dark* from Bella Books, and *Naughty Spanking Stories 2* from Pretty Things Press).

In 2005, she received a Goldie award from the Golden Crown Literary Society in both the Romance (*Fated Love*) and Intrigue/Action/Mystery categories (*Justice in the Shadows*) and in 2003/2004, the Alice B. award for her body of work. A member of the GCLS, Pink Ink, and the Romance Writers of America, she lives with her partner, Lee, in Wayne, PA where she both writes and heads Bold Strokes Books, a lesbian publishing company.

Her upcoming works include selections in *Lessons in Love: Erotic Interludes 3* from Bold Strokes Books, from Bella Books (2006), the next novel in the Honor series, *Honor Reclaimed* (December 2005), the romance *Turn Back Time* (March 2006), and *Promising Hearts* (June 2006) the sequel to *Innocent Hearts*.

Look for information about these works at www.boldstrokesbooks. com.

Books Available From Bold Strokes Books

Innocent Hearts by Radclyffe. In a wild and unforgiving land, two women learn about love, passion, and the wonders of the heart. (1-933110-21-X)

The Temple at Landfall by Jane Fletcher. An imprinter, one of Celaeno's most revered servants of the Goddess, is also a prisoner to the faith—until a Ranger frees her by claiming her heart. (1-933110-27-9)

Force of Nature by Kim Baldwin. From tornados to forest fires, the forces of nature conspire to bring Gable McCoy and Erin Richards close to danger, and closer to each other. (1-933110-23-6)

In Too Deep by Ronica Black. Undercover homicide cop Erin McKenzie tracks a femme fatale who just might be a real killer…with love and danger hot on her heels. (1-933110-17-1)

Stolen Moments: *Erotic Interludes 2* by Stacia Seaman and Radclyffe, eds. Love on the run, in the office, in the shadows…Fast, furious, and almost too hot to handle. (1-933110-16-3)

Course of Action by Gun Brooke. Actress Carolyn Black desperately wants the starring role in an upcoming film produced by Annelie Peterson. Just how far will she go for the dream part of a lifetime? (1-933110-22-8)

Rangers at Roadsend by Jane Fletcher. Sergeant Chip Coppelli has learned to spot trouble coming, and that is exactly what she sees in her new recruit, Katryn Nagata. The Celaeno series. (1-933110-28-7)

Justice Served by Radclyffe. Lieutenant Rebecca Frye and her lover, Dr. Catherine Rawlings, embark on a deadly game of hide-and-seek with an underworld kingpin who traffics in human souls. (1-933110-15-5)

Distant Shores, Silent Thunder by Radclyffe. Dr. Tory King—along with the women who love her—is forced to examine the boundaries of love, friendship, and the ties that transcend time. (1-933110-08-2)

Hunter's Pursuit by Kim Baldwin. A raging blizzard, a mountain hideaway, and a killer-for-hire set a scene for disaster—or desire—when Katarzyna Demetrious rescues a beautiful stranger. (1-933110-09-0)

The Walls of Westernfort by Jane Fletcher. All Temple Guard Natasha Ionadis wants is to serve the Goddess—until she falls in love with one of the rebels she is sworn to destroy. The Celaeno series. (1-933110-24-4)

Change Of Pace: *Erotic Interludes* by Radclyffe. Twenty-five hot-wired encounters guaranteed to spark more than just your imagination. Erotica as you've always dreamed of it. (1-933110-07-4)

Honor Guards by Radclyffe. In a wild flight for their lives, the president's daughter and those who are sworn to protect her wage a desperate struggle for survival. (1-933110-01-5)

Fated Love by Radclyffe. Amidst the chaos and drama of a busy emergency room, two women must contend not only with the fragile nature of life, but also with the irresistible forces of fate. (1-933110-05-8)

Justice in the Shadows by Radclyffe. In a shadow world of secrets and lies, Detective Sergeant Rebecca Frye and her lover, Dr. Catherine Rawlings, join forces in the elusive search for justice. (1-933110-03-1)

shadowland by Radclyffe. In a world on the far edge of desire, two women are drawn together by power, passion, and dark pleasures. An erotic romance. (1-933110-11-2)

Love's Masquerade by Radclyffe. Plunged into the indistinguishable realms of fiction, fantasy, and hidden desires, Auden Frost is forced to question all she believes about the nature of love. (1-933110-14-7)

Love & Honor by Radclyffe. The president's daughter and her lover are faced with difficult choices as they battle a tangled web of Washington intrigue for...love and honor. (1-933110-10-4)

Beyond the Breakwater by Radclyffe. One Provincetown summer three women learn the true meaning of love, friendship, and family. (1-933110-06-6)

Tomorrow's Promise by Radclyffe. One timeless summer, two very different women discover the power of passion to heal and the promise of hope that only love can bestow. (1-933110-12-0)

Love's Tender Warriors by Radclyffe. Two women who have accepted loneliness as a way of life learn that love is worth fighting for and a battle they cannot afford to lose. (1-933110-02-3)

Love's Melody Lost by Radclyffe. A secretive artist with a haunted past and a young woman escaping a life that has proved to be a lie find their destinies entwined. (1-933110-00-7)

Safe Harbor by Radclyffe. A mysterious newcomer, a reclusive doctor, and a troubled gay teenager learn about love, friendship, and trust during one tumultuous summer in Provincetown. (1-933110-13-9)

Above All, Honor by Radclyffe. Secret Service Agent Cameron Roberts fights her desire for the one woman she can't have—Blair Powell, the daughter of the president of the United States. (1-933110-04-X)